BAYOU HEAT

ALEXANDRA IVY

LAURA WRIGHT

Sebastian/Aristide
By Alexandra Ivy and Laura Wright
Copyright © 2013 Laura Wright and Debbie Raleigh

Cover Art by Patricia Schmitt (Pickyme)
Digital Layout by www.formatting4U.com

This book is a work of fiction. The names, characters, places, and incidents are products of the writer's imagination or have been used fictitiously and are not to be construed as real. Any resemblance to persons, living or dead, actual events, locales or organizations is entirely coincidental.

All rights reserved. With the exception of quotes used in reviews, this book may not be reproduced or used in whole or in part by any means existing without written permission from the author.

SEBASTIAN

ALEXANDRA IVY

SEBASTIAN
ALEXANDRA IVY

PROLOGUE

The small cabin with a thatched roof wasn't a traditional prison. There were no bars. No locks. No uniformed guards.

Instead, it was hidden on an isolated island in the Wildlands, surrounded by thick, untamed foliage and a treacherous bog that could kill the unwary. Just outside the door, several large Pantera in cat form stood on constant guard. But it was the magic of the elders which ensured that no one was going in or out of the small structure.

It was a place that only a handful of Pantera even realized existed. They didn't need to know, because it was where those Pantera who lost control of their cats and became feral were taken to be put to death.

Not precisely a tourist attraction.

Today, however, it housed a far more dangerous predator than a crazed panther.

The ultimate evil.

And the Wildlands would never be the same.

***

Inside the cabin, Shakpi sat on the narrow cot that

was the only furnishing in the room.

She didn't care about the stifling heat, or the bugs that crawled over the dirt floor.

In fact, she rejoiced in them.

After what felt like an eternity of being trapped beneath the Wildlands, she had broken out of the prison her sister, Opela, had created by sacrificing her own life. Now she savored the sensation of freedom.

Oh, she hadn't entirely escaped. Opela's magic had effectively bound her to this land…the bitch. But over the past century, Shakpi had slowly and patiently weakened the edges of the prison. Once she could touch the world, she began calling her human slaves, using them to spread her infection that started the slow destruction of the Wildlands. As her power grew she could begin to manipulate the Pantera themselves, using them as pawns in their own annihilation.

Still, she remained stuck, her incorporeal form trapped by her sister's spell.

It wasn't until the Shaman had started to use his skills to contact his ancestors that she realized she could tap into his connection to the dead. Carefully she began infusing a small part of herself into the human male. The spell that had held her captive was meant to recognize the power of a goddess, not a human. She was slowly camouflaging herself in the guise of the Shaman.

It'd taken years. But Shakpi had learned to be patient. Even when the Shaman had seemingly disappeared just when she was prepared to complete her transformation. She knew he would return.

Her destiny was to rule the world.

SEBASTIAN
ALEXANDRA IVY

It was written in the stars.

And her faith had been rewarded. Just a few hours ago the man had reappeared in the Wildlands, arrogantly opening himself to her possession. Fool.

Unfortunately, she hadn't quite anticipated the downside of being sheathed in a human form.

Not until she'd been so rudely attacked by the Pantera.

It was only then that she realized that while she was immortal, her new body was vulnerable to damage. Which was the only reason she was currently trapped in the cabin instead of destroying the bastards who'd dared to try and kill her.

Thankfully she was able to use her powers to hold off the initial rush of Pantera, managing to kill at least a half dozen before they'd driven her into this tiny cell and retreated.

No doubt they were even now debating how to kill a goddess without losing more of their warriors, but Shakpi wasn't particularly worried. At least not about escaping from the cabin. She had telepathically linked with one of her disciples who was swiftly approaching to release her.

Her only concern was how she was going to complete her destruction of the Wildlands.

The human form she was forced to use was too fragile to allow her to use the full might of her powers. And worse, it was susceptible to injury.

She glanced down at her male body that was covered by bloody clothing.

The deep gashes that had nearly sliced off the arms and one leg were healing, thanks to her magic, but it would take days before the pathetically weak body would be fully recovered.

Clearly she would have to find another way to complete her revenge.

Starting with an army.

And speaking of an army…

Shakpi rose to her feet as she heard the soft sound of voices outside the door. It seemed her rescue had arrived.

There was a brief delay as if the approaching Pantera was being questioned about his right to enter the cabin. Then at last, Shakpi could detect the fading scent of her guards.

A smile curled her lips, or rather the lips of Chayton, as the door was pushed open and the male Hunter entered the cramped room.

"Hello, Hiss." The words echoed through the air, filled with a power that proved she was no human. "Be the first to welcome your goddess into the world."

SEBASTIAN
ALEXANDRA IVY

CHAPTER 1

The Suits' private headquarters near the center of the Wildlands looked more like a mansion from "Gone With The Wind" than an office building. A sweeping Colonial-style structure, it was painted white with black shutters, and had six fluted columns that held up the second-story balcony.

Inside, however, it was a buzzing hub of activity, filled with the sort of high-tech equipment usually reserved for the military. Pantera Diplomats often used the Geeks to hack and spy and infiltrate the human world. It was the easiest way to keep track of their enemies.

Then there were the Suits who preferred to do their job the old-fashioned way.

By getting their hands dirty.

And no one was better at getting his hands dirty than Sebastian Duval.

A tall male with bronze skin, he had a chiseled body that was currently covered by a pair of black chinos and a white silk shirt left open at the neck. He had pale green eyes swirled with yellow that most women called hazel, and tawny hair threaded with gold that brushed his broad shoulders.

He had a sophisticated gloss that allowed him to move among humans without them sensing that a lethal animal prowled just below his skin.

It was a skill that had served him well over the past century as fewer and fewer people remembered the presence of the strange puma shifters that lived in the deepest part of the bayous. Now they were mere myths to all but the highest human government officials who had agreed to keep their presence wrapped in secrecy.

Or at least their presence had been a secret until two weeks ago.

Prowling from one end of the long room that held a half dozen desks and a line of monitors on the paneled wall, Sebastian had a phone pressed to his ear, rapidly reassuring the governor of Arkansas that there wasn't a feral pack of Pantera ravaging their way across the country.

Christ…it was a pain in his ass.

He didn't know who or what was behind the strange attacks that had started in New Orleans and were rapidly spreading across the South. And he was pissed as hell that he was being forced to waste time dealing with hysterical politicians who'd somehow gotten a bug up their asses that there were wild pumas hunting innocent humans.

Idiots.

He needed to be concentrating his attention on the hunt for Shakpi, or even helping the warriors to prepare for the coming war.

And there would be a war…there was no doubt about that.

Now that the goddess had been released from her prison it was only a matter of time before she tried to destroy the Pantera.

Offering his solemn promise that he would give his full cooperation to the governor, Sebastian ended his call just as Raphael stepped through the open door.

Instantly a silence filled the room.

The head of the Suits was that kind of man. It wasn't his golden good looks or his large body, or even the arrogance etched onto his lean face that captured and held attention of the dozen Pantera. He was, quite simply, a natural born leader who commanded respect.

Today his expression was grim as he glanced around the gathered Pantera. "Clear the room," he barked.

Sebastian felt a stab of concern as the men and women swiftly exited by a side door, leaving him alone with the older man.

Two good things had come out of Shakpi's escape. The first was that the rot that had been destroying the Wildlands had suddenly stopped spreading. And the second was the fact that Raphael's mate, Ashe, was no longer fighting for her life, or the life of their unborn cub.

Or at least, she hadn't been the last time he'd checked in with his leader.

Now his heart slammed against his ribs as he studied his companion's stark expression.

"Ashe?" he rasped, barely daring to breathe until Raphael flashed a reassuring smile.

"Is well."

"Thank god," Sebastian breathed. Ashe was not only Raphael's mate, but she was currently carrying the first Pantera child in over fifty years.

A priceless treasure they would all protect with their lives.

"No, thank Isi," Raphael muttered.

Sebastian arched a brow. Isi was Ashe's long-lost sister, and since her arrival the infection or poison or whatever it was that had been slowly killing the fragile young woman had nearly disappeared.

"You believe she's responsible for your mate's recovery?"

Raphael folded his arms over his chest. "No doubt in my mind."

"So why does she remain in isolation?"

"Because the elders refuse to admit they could be wrong." Disgust laced his words. "They are convinced that she is destined to destroy the Wildlands. And they have enough influence to sway a large number of our people."

"The rumor is that Isi's blood did scorch the earth," Sebastian said, repeating the gossip that was swirling among the Pantera.

"Isi isn't the danger," Raphael snapped, clearly not there to discuss the mystery of his sister-in-law. "We have to be united if we are to defeat Shakpi."

Sebastian shivered. No one asked the question of how exactly they were going to achieve that little miracle.

Not when no one had the answer.

"True." Sebastian had been a witness to the moment Chayton, the human Shaman, had tried to close his connection to the trapped goddess. In fact, Sebastian had more than one scar from the fierce battle when they'd realized that Chayton had been possessed by Shakpi. "Have you located the Shaman?"

"No, but Parish has his Hunters on the trail."

Sebastian nodded, a familiar ball of frustration lodged in the pit of his stomach. "I'd give my left nut to know how the bastard escaped."

"No shit." Raphael rammed his fingers through his hair, a low growl rumbling in his chest. "I'm still trying to sort through that little clusterfuck."

Sebastian grimaced, not envying his friend's job. There were at least ten different stories of who was supposed to be where when it was discovered their prisoner had escaped.

"If this isn't about Ashe or Chayton, then what has you in such a twit?"

Raphael narrowed his golden gaze. "Twit?"

"Twit. Snit." Sebastian shrugged. "A mood."

"I'm a Pantera." Raphael peeled back his lips to reveal his elongated fangs. "I don't have moods."

Sebastian snorted. "And I'm about to sprout wings and flap around the room."

Raphael pulled out his phone, searching for a webpage before shoving it into Sebastian's hand.

"Read."

Sebastian glanced down, scanning the front page of a prominent New Orleans newspaper. His brows snapped together at the lurid headline:

LOCAL WOMAN MAULED, AUTHORITIES ON HIGH ALERT

"Shit." Sebastian gave an annoyed shake of his head. "Another wild animal attack?"

"It gets worse. Keep reading."

With a growing sense of dread, Sebastian skimmed through the short article.

"Pantera," he snarled, rereading the last paragraph to make sure he hadn't misread the shocking claim. Nope. There it was: the female was convinced that she was attacked by a Pantera. "How? Only top human officials are aware the Pantera truly exist. Which is bad enough." He made a sound of disgust. "I've spent all morning on the phone with the governor of Arkansas."

Raphael grimaced. "It could be that the humans are remembering the stories of their grandparents. When they're frightened, they often turn to myth and legend."

Sebastian didn't need to be a Diplomat to know that Raphael didn't believe this was a random accusation made out of fear.

"Or?" he prompted.

"Or traitors have been whispering our name among the masses."

"Damn." Sebastian understood better than anyone this new, unexpected danger. It was bad enough to be outed just when they were threatened with extinction. But to be revealed and then blamed for the violent attacks was a guaranteed way to make enemies of the humans. "What do you want from me?"

Raphael reached for his phone, stabbing a finger at the screen. "I want this stopped."

Sebastian blinked in surprise, anticipation heating

his blood. Damn. It'd been far too long since he'd been on the hunt.

"Not that I'm not ready and willing to kill the bastards, but you don't usually give me the opportunity to release my inner cat."

"And you're going to have to keep it leashed." Raphael squashed his brief hope for a taste of blood. "At least for now. The FBI are demanding answers."

Sebastian grudgingly bridled his eager cat, forcing himself to return to his role as Diplomat. As much as his animal side longed for a good fight, he preferred to avoid violence whenever possible. Besides, they had Hunters who were trained to kick ass.

"I bet they are," he said dryly, already considering his various contacts in New Orleans. "I have someone in the mayor's office who can smooth things over."

Raphael shook his head. "Not this time."

Sebastian stiffened. He didn't have to be a psychic to know he wasn't going to like what Raphael had to say.

"What do you mean?"

"The human officials have demanded that we work together to discover who's instigating the trouble."

Nope. He didn't like it.

Not even a little.

"They can demand whatever they want," he growled.

Raphael held up a warning hand. "We need to cooperate."

"Since when?"

"Since our presence has gone from being fiction to fact."

Sebastian clenched his teeth in frustration. He understood that it made sense to work with the human authorities. Until they knew who was behind this, the Pantera had to foster all the goodwill possible.

But that didn't make it any less annoying.

"It would be easier to track down the villains responsible for the attacks without the interference of the FBI."

Raphael's eyes glowed with the power of his cat, revealing he wasn't any happier than Sebastian.

"I agree, but the public are swiftly becoming convinced that we're a threat to their safety and we both know what happens when fear rules among humans."

"Mob mentality," Sebastian muttered.

"Exactly."

Sebastian paced toward the large window that overlooked the communal meadow where the Pantera often gathered for meals. Surrounded by trees draped with Spanish moss and bathed in the early autumn sunlight, the Wildlands was a place of peace.

Home.

Instinctively his gaze moved toward the clinic that was barely visible through the trees. His parents were both Healers. Gentle souls who were so deeply committed to their vocation they wouldn't harm another creature, even if they were being attacked.

It was his duty to protect them.

Whether he wanted to work with the humans or not.

"Shit." He turned back to meet Raphael's bleak expression. "Is there more?"

The older man reached into his back pocket to pull out a folded piece of paper, handing it to Sebastian.

"This is your contact."

Sebastian read the name scribbled on the paper. "Reny Smith?" He scowled in confusion. "Never heard of her. They're sticking me with some damned rookie?"

"She's coming in from New York."

The knowledge didn't appease his irritation. There were a handful of agents who had high enough clearance to be aware of the Pantera. It didn't make sense to bring in a stranger.

"Why?"

"She's supposedly an expert in interrogations."

Sebastian made a sound of disgust. He knew the seedy underbelly of human politics.

"As if I need a human to help me with interrogations."

"Be nice."

"Is that an order?"

Raphael allowed his cat to prowl close to the surface, the air heating with his power. "Yes."

"Shit."

***

Reny Smith ignored the glances of the local agents who strolled past the small conference room that she'd claimed as her office.

She'd known she would be the subject of curiosity and even resentment when she'd asked for an opportunity to work on this case.

She had all the ingredients to piss off the local boys club.

She was an outsider. She was a woman. And she was barely out of Quantico.

Still, she'd been oddly convinced that she could help to sort through the mangled stories and hysterical accusations before the situation escalated into public panic. Even after her boss had granted her the top secret clearance and grudgingly confessed that the ancient stories were true. That there were real life puma shifters who lived in the bayous, and that she would have to work with one of them.

Well, she would work with him if he ever bothered to make an appearance.

Clicking her tongue with impatience, Reny rose to her feet, smoothing her hands down the black jacket that matched her slacks, and paced toward the window overlooking the majestic Lake Pontchartrain.

It was a mesmerizing sight with the sunset painting the water in vivid shades of pink and lilac. Of course, everything about New Orleans was mesmerizing.

No doubt it was because it was a city of such intense contradictions.

The decadent mixture of old world charm and modern high-rises. The sound of sweet jazz that filled the air, lacing its way among the dark, grinding poverty that lurked just out of sight. The aroma of chicory coffee overlaid with the earthy scent of the bayous.

It all combined to create a feast for the senses.

Reny told herself that was the cause for the restlessness that had plagued her since her plane had landed two days ago.

It didn't entirely make sense. But it was the best explanation she had for the weird feeling that something inside her was struggling to get out.

Besides, over the past years she'd become adept at telling herself small lies.

Her superior speed was just a matter of training. She was stronger than she should be because of genetics. Her unnerving ability to tell when people were lying to her was a god-given talent.

And that feeling that she was somehow more aware of the world around her? Well, she'd built a shield in her mind that allowed her to lock out her acute awareness so she could pretend to be just like everyone else.

What else could she do?

Ever since she'd awakened in a New York hospital eight years ago with complete amnesia, she'd felt like a freak. If she actually accepted she was different on a fundamental level, then...

Then she wouldn't just feel like a freak, she'd become one.

She abruptly shivered, rubbing her arms as electric tingles raced over her skin.

There was something approaching. No, not something...someone.

Feeling a ridiculous sense of premonition, Reny slowly turned, her breath wrenched from her lungs.

Holy...shit.

The man filling the doorway was drop-dead, heart-stopping, get-him-naked-now gorgeous.

Her gaze did a lingering inventory, starting with the thick, tawny hair that was pulled into a tail at his nape, moving over the bronzed male features and down the hard, perfectly sculpted body shown to advantage in black chino slacks and white shirt.

Her dazzled gaze returned to his gorgeous face, her heart slamming against her ribs.

Those eyes…she'd never seen anything like them. A green as pale as spring grass with yellow swirls that seemed to glow in the fading light.

Pantera, a voice whispered through her mind.

It didn't take the memory of her boss explaining that the age-old stories were true to warn her that this male was one of the elusive puma shifters.

Or even his inhuman beauty.

She could physically *feel* the cat that crawled beneath the surface.

"You're Reny Smith?" he murmured, his voice whiskey smooth with a hint of a southern drawl.

The sound of it wrapped around her like heated honey, warming places that shouldn't be warmed in public.

Damn.

Something stirred deep inside her. Not just the strange restlessness that had been plaguing her, but an aching need that was suddenly ignited in the pit of her stomach.

She determinedly squared her shoulders. What was wrong with her?

This was her big opportunity.

She wasn't going to blow it because this man was making her squirm with unfamiliar sensations.

"I am. I assume you're Mr.—"

"Sebastian," he interrupted, prowling across the institutional gray carpet to stand directly in front of her.

Heat licked over her skin.

"You're late."

The yellow in his eyes deepened to gold as his gaze skimmed down to where her white blouse was opened just enough to give a hint of her breasts.

"Actually, I would say I'm just in time," he murmured.

Reny should have rolled her eyes. She'd learned to ignore the typical male response to her looks since entering the academy.

Now, however, she was instantly on the defensive.

"Look, I'm here to work. If you…" She stiffened as he leaned forward, his nose flaring as if he were dragging in her scent. "What?"

"They told me you were human," he growled softly.

"Human?" She blinked in confusion. "What the hell are you talking about?"

"I can smell your cat."

A cold chill inched down her spine as she met his unnerving gaze. "Is that supposed to be some kind of joke?"

A tawny brow flicked upward. "Why would it be a joke?"

"I don't know what you think you smell, but I can

assure you I don't even own a cat." The words had barely left her mouth when he'd closed the small space between them and pressed his nose to the curve of her neck. She sucked in a terrified breath. Not because she was frightened of the overtly beautiful man. But because his touch was sending jolts of savage arousal through her trembling body. "Please don't," she husked.

"I'm not going to hurt you, sugar," he drawled, allowing his lips to trail down her throat, lingering over the frantic beat of her pulse before he slowly straightened, his searching gaze sweeping over her face. "I assume you have a reason for your charade."

Attempting to squash her panic, Reny stepped around his large body and headed toward the door. She'd prepared herself for a rough, ill-mannered lout. Someone more animal than man. Not this gorgeous, sophisticated stranger who was making her skin feel as if it was too tight for her body.

"I don't think this is going to work."

"Stop."

The command in his voice had something inside her instantly halting her retreat, slowly turning to face him.

The fact that she'd obeyed pissed her off. "Don't give me orders, Mr.—"

"Sebastian," he smoothly reminded her, his beautiful face unreadable. "I thought you requested to be the FBI liaison?"

She scowled. "I asked to be given the opportunity to use my training."

"And at the first hurdle you're willing to walk away?"

The prickles continued the race through her body,

her heart beating way too fast. "You're a massively large hurdle," she retorted.

His smile was filled with sin. "Oh, sugar, you have no idea."

"That's it."

She turned back toward the door, but before she could take a step he was standing directly in front of her.

Holy shit. Just how fast could he move?

"Let's start again," he murmured, holding up his hands as if to convince her he was harmless. Yeah. The very air sizzled with danger. "Please, tell me what you've managed to discover."

Reny wavered. Common sense told her to walk away. She didn't precisely understand why being in the same room with this man was making her so edgy, and she suspected that it was better not to know.

But the part that had allowed her to survive waking in a sterile hospital with no name, no family, and no past refused to allow her to quit.

He was right. If she allowed the first obstacle to send her scuttling back to New York then she might as well give up her career, because she'd never get another opportunity to prove herself.

Stiffening her spine, Reny crossed toward the long table at the side of the room where she'd spread out her files.

She'd never been a coward. She wasn't going to start now.

"I've interviewed the female who claims to have been attacked by the..." She fumbled over the word. "Pantera."

Moving in near silence, Sebastian was abruptly standing at her side, his heat wrapping around her with seductive force.

"Claims?" he demanded.

Reny clenched her teeth. Dammit. She would not shiver. Or whimper. Or melt into a puddle at his Italian leather shoes.

"She was lying."

"How do you know?"

Good question.

She had no intention of sharing the truth.

"I'm very skilled in reading body language," she said.

"I bet," he drawled, almost as if he knew her little secret. "No wonder you're an expert in interrogations."

"Yes." She deliberately stepped away from his intoxicating heat.

Not that it helped.

Sebastian's presence consumed every inch of the room.

"If it wasn't a Pantera that caused her wounds, then what did?" he asked. "And more importantly, why did she lie?"

"She was paid."

CHAPTER 2

Sebastian's cat prowled anxiously beneath his skin.

What the hell was going on?

Was Reny Smith pretending to be a human to infiltrate the FBI? Was she one of the traitors?

Or did she truly not realize she was Pantera?

The vital questions should have consumed him, but instead he couldn't think beyond the intense awareness that had punched into him the moment he'd walked through the door.

God. Damn.

He didn't know what was setting him on fire.

Was it the dark hair streaked with fiery highlights that begged to be freed from her tight ponytail? The pale oval face that was dominated by a pair of moss green eyes? The slender, athletic body she tried to hide beneath the black suit? The rich, exotic scent of her cat?

All he knew was that he was barely leashing the urge to toss her onto the long table and strip away those starchy clothes and lick her from head to toe.

His cat purred at the thought of spreading her legs and lapping up her spicy arousal that was already perfuming the air. Her human mind might be wary of the desire that was setting off sparks between them, but her cat was ready and eager.

The only thing halting him was the knowledge that he couldn't be sure this female wasn't a trap.

"Do you have proof?" he demanded, forcing himself to concentrate on his reason for traveling to New Orleans.

Eventually he would figure out the puzzle that was Reny Smith.

And when he did, he'd have his aching cock buried so deeply inside her she'd be screaming in pleasure.

Perhaps sensing his brutal hunger, Reny inched away to grab a file from the neat stack on the table. Then, sucking in a steadying breath, she flipped it open to reveal a stack of photos.

"No, but look."

Sebastian allowed her the small space. For now.

"What am I seeing?" He reached to spread out the photos.

"This is Koni Handler's apartment." Reny pointed to the shabby brick building that was squeezed between a laundromat and an abandoned bookstore. She moved her finger to a photo of a cramped living room. "She shared it with three other girls. Her portion of the rent was three-fifty a month."

"It's not the best neighborhood," he said. "It could have been a local thug who attacked her. That would explain why she tried to make up a wild story. She couldn't risk the truth."

Reny shook her head, shuffling through the photos to reveal one of a pretty, dark-haired woman.

She looked to be in her early twenties, although there was a hardness in her dark eyes and a petulant curve to her lips that hinted that she'd seen more than most females her age.

"Now, this is her at the police station."

Sebastian was confused. Reny had shown him the apartment, but not the actual crime scene, and the pictures of the victim didn't reveal the wounds from her supposed attack.

"I think it will save us time if you just tell me what I should be looking for."

Reny tapped the photo. "This is a Coach bag. Retail it costs five hundred dollars," she said. "Her jacket is Gucci." Her finger moved to point at the woman's diamond earrings. "And those earrings are at least a carat."

"They could be knockoffs."

"Are you kidding?" She sent him a disbelieving glance. "I'm from New York."

"And?"

"I could spot a fake at a hundred paces."

He hid a smile. Sassy. He liked it.

"I also recognize an original when I see it," he murmured, allowing his gaze to sweep over her exquisite face before returning his attention to the photo. "Maybe she has a sugar daddy."

She cleared her throat, her face flushed with an excitement she was desperately trying to hide.

"If she does, he has to be new," she said. "She pawned her laptop last week to pay her share of the rent."

Sassy and smart.

His cat preened with pleasure.

"Good catch." He brushed the back of his fingers over her cheek. "I think I should speak with this Koni."

She shivered before she was abruptly yanking from his touch, her chin tilting to a militant angle.

"We."

"We." His cat purred. "I like the sound of that."

She rolled her eyes, reaching for her purse on the table. "My car's in the lot."

He followed a step behind her as she headed for the door, enjoying the view of her tight little ass.

Soon he intended to be cupping that fine booty in his hands as she rode him to paradise.

Fully erect, he ignored the curious glances as they headed toward the back of the building. So far as he knew, only Reny and the top brass realized that he was a Pantera, but humans instinctively reacted to his power.

Men hurried to step out of his path, while females did their best to capture his attention.

His gaze never strayed from Reny's delectable backside. "What if I want to drive?"

Reny stepped into the elevator, waiting for the doors to close before shooting him a smoldering glare.

"I don't let any man take me for a ride."

With a fluid speed, he had her backed against the paneled wall of the elevator, his hands bracketing her shoulders as he leaned down to stroke his lips down the vulnerable curve of her throat.

"Oh, sugar, don't ever challenge a Pantera," he husked, drowning in her spicy scent. "We bite."

She shivered, but it wasn't fear sending tremors through her body.

Still, she held herself rigid, refusing to acknowledge the heat that simmered in her moss green eyes.

"Are you trying to frighten me?" she rasped.

He nipped the skin above her racing pulse. It was nothing more than the smallest taste, but the essence of her exploded on his tongue.

A growl rumbled in his chest.

"Just giving you fair warning."

He could sense the storm of emotions that battled inside her.

Fear. Confusion. And a hunger so fierce it dampened her skin in a fine layer of sweat.

But with a willpower he could only admire, she kept her brittle composure intact.

"Then let me return the favor. I always carry a Taser in my purse," she warned, lifting her hands to press them against his chest. "Move back."

Sebastian instantly dropped his arms and stepped away. He would push, but he would never force.

It was only a matter of time before Reny gave herself freely.

"Aggressive." He flashed his most charming smile. "I like it."

She muttered a curse beneath her breath. "Do you ever stop?"

"No." Not when it came to this female.

Sebastian pulled his cellphone from his pocket as they left the building and slid into the standard midsize cop car. He not only wanted to update Raphael on

Reny's suspicions, but he intended to discover just what sort of game the female FBI agent was playing.

With his various texts at last sent, he slid the phone back into his pocket and studied the pure line of Reny's profile, his cat restlessly stirring beneath his skin. His animal didn't understand being so close to this delectable female and not being allowed to touch. It was the increasingly dismal homes that lined the narrow street that at last jerked him out of his brooding thoughts. They weren't far from their destination.

"Can you park a few blocks from the apartment building?"

She sent him a startled glance. "Why?"

"I want to see if I can catch any scent of Pantera in the area."

Without hesitation, Reny slowed the car, pulling into a loading zone next to the curb. Sebastian hid a satisfied smile. She instinctively trusted him.

Even when she wanted to kick him in the nuts.

He had a premonition that very soon he was going to need that faith.

"I'll drop you off here and park around the corner." She nodded toward the north. "The apartment building is at the end of the next block. I'll wait in the lobby."

He stepped out of the car, sending her a teasing grin. "There won't be any waiting."

"Arrogant ass," she muttered as he jogged away.

"I can hear you, sugar," he called.

"I know, dumpling," she called back.

He chuckled, anticipation sizzling through his body.

Oh, Special Agent Reny Smith, you are playing with fire…

***

Shakpi had to admit there were unexpected benefits to possessing a human form.

She'd discovered a passion for the spicy gumbo that she ordered from a local restaurant, as well as an addiction to the sugar-coated beignets that she demanded every morning.

There was also the unexpected pleasure that could be found between the talented lips of her devoted disciple.

Seated in the library of the large mansion that was built along the bluffs of the Mississippi River, she gave a low groan as she climaxed into the female's mouth. Who knew a cock could be the source of such pleasure?

There was the sound of the door being pushed open, then a small gasp as a woman with silver hair pulled into a bun and wearing a loose cotton dress stepped into the room.

"Oh." The face leathered by years in the hot Louisiana sun twisted into an expression of disgust. "Forgive me."

"Enter," Shakpi snapped, motioning away the disciple kneeling between her legs so she could rise to her feet and pull up her pants. She felt no embarrassment, only irritation that she'd been kept waiting. "You're late."

With the clanking from the dozens of bracelets

that lined the voodoo priestess's scrawny arms, she moved across the wooden floor.

"I was forced to walk from the highway."

Shakpi narrowed her gaze. It had been an easy task to find a suitable lair and kill the humans who were currently occupying it, but she'd discovered that while there were a handful of benefits to her physical body, there were far more disadvantages.

She was weak, vulnerable to injury and she had an acute reaction to the stench of human technology.

The sooner she could find the means to release her spirit from the bonds of the mortal form, the sooner she could rule the world.

"I dislike the smell of fumes," she snapped, her gaze flicking dismissively over Lady Cerise. The woman possessed an arrogance that Shakpi was eager to shatter. "I also dislike being kept waiting. Don't allow it to happen again."

"I told you—"

The chandelier above them swayed, a crack forming in the cove ceiling. "You have been a dedicated disciple, Cerise." Shakpi's male voice held a quiet, deadly warning that couldn't be mistaken. "It would be a shame to have to destroy you now."

Cerise fell to her knees, her head bowed. "I am your servant."

"Hmm." Shakpi strolled forward, savoring the spiky fear that filled the air. "So you say."

"I have proven my loyalty," the priestess insisted, her head still lowered. "I have gathered disciples to spread your infection through the Wildlands. I have devoted years to searching for the Shaman to help open your pathway—"

"And yet, I still wait for the war you promised."

"The opening battle has begun."

Shakpi made a sound of disgust. She'd read the reports of the escalating violent attacks spreading across the South, and the rumors that had started to spread about the rabid puma shifters who were crawling out of the swamps to hunt humans. But she wanted instant results.

"Do you know how long I've waited to see the Pantera destroyed?"

"Which is why we must not risk your ultimate success by pressing too hard, too fast," Cerise urged, her body tense. "The humans are becoming increasingly fearful. Once they believe their local officials can't protect them it will be a simple matter to push them into violence."

"Don't fail me, Cerise." Shakpi reached down to grab the female by the neck, lifting her off her feet and squeezing hard enough to make her moan with pain. "You won't like what I do to disciples who prove themselves to be unworthy."

***

Reny took her time strolling along the street, despite the fact that dusk was cloaking the buildings in shadows.

She was a well-trained agent with a gun tucked in a holster beneath her jacket. Besides, she'd never had the trouble of many women. Men might leer and whistle and harass her from a distance, but none of them tried to get into her private space.

It was almost as if they were…intimidated by her.

Until Sebastian Duval.

She absently wiped her damp hands down her slacks, trying to concentrate on her surroundings. She could sometimes get a vibe from a crime scene and the neighborhood around it.

Tonight, however, she couldn't concentrate on anything but the nagging ache in the pit of her stomach.

Dammit.

She'd hoped that a little space would allow her to shake off the disturbing arousal that scorched through her. But ridiculously, it only seemed to grow worse.

It didn't make sense.

She never noticed guys. Not because she was some man-hater. It was just that she'd been so focused on her career that she'd never had time to play the games other women seemed to enjoy.

But from the second that Sebastian had strolled into the room her entire body had been on fire. As if he'd tossed a match on her long-dormant libido.

Okay, he was gorgeous.

No, wait. He was way beyond gorgeous. Reny wasn't certain there was a word that could capture his tawny beauty. Or the incandescent animal magnetism that the designer clothes and polished charm did nothing to mute.

But he was annoying, and arrogant, and clearly demented if he thought for a second he could make her believe she had some sort of cat smell.

Oh yeah, and there was the little fact that he

wasn't even human.

If he weren't her current partner and vital to her future success, she would...

The image of what she wanted to do to him seared through her mind.

That long, chiseled body stretched across her hotel bed. His bronzed skin glistening with a light sheen of perspiration. His hair tousled and his hazel eyes darkened with pleasure as she kissed a path down his stomach to the hard cock...

She gave a strangled sound, a heat staining her cheeks.

Where the hell did that come from?

The answer hit her as she rounded the corner to discover Tall, Tawny and Tantalizing leaning against the apartment building.

Her nerve endings tingled as if they'd been scrubbed raw, as she studied the predatory male. Even wrapped in dusk he commanded full attention, creating chaos among the group of women walking down the sidewalk as they tripped over their feet at the sight of him.

Oddly annoyed by the lingering female glances, Reny moved to stand at his side, her brows pulled together.

"How did you..." She cut off her words as a smug smile curved his lips. "Never mind."

With a shake of her head she turned to pull open the door to the apartment building, stepping into the lobby.

Sebastian was directly on her heels, moving around her to investigate the bleak space. Across the peeling linoleum floor was the elevator, as well as the narrow door to the stairs. Opposite were a dozen mailboxes built into the wall. And closer to the door was an orange couch that she'd bet had been there since The Brady Bunch was on the air.

Reny shuddered. Had anyone actually sat on those lumpy cushions in the past decade?

"The attack supposedly happened here?" Sebastian demanded.

"Yes," she said, watching him pace from one end of the lobby to the other with a lethal grace that was mesmerizing.

"Cameras?"

She pointed toward the hole cut in the ceiling near the flickering florescent lights. "The owner of the building said they were temporarily out of service, but I suspect they've never functioned."

Sebastian nodded, crouching next to the mailboxes. "There's blood, but no scent of Pantera."

"It happened three days ago," she pointed out.

He straightened, turning to meet her guarded gaze. "After such a violent encounter there should be some trace of the attacker."

"Unless he could mask his scent."

"Impossible." Irritation emphasized the yellow-gold in his amazing eyes. "Just as the wounds on the female are impossible."

"Why?"

"A Pantera can't shift into his animal form unless he's in the Wildlands."

Reny hesitated. Her briefing had been lacking any details about the Pantera. No doubt because there wasn't much information to share.

The puma shifters had been elusive for so long that even the rumors of their abilities had died away.

"Are you telling me the truth?"

He shrugged. "It would serve no purpose for me to lie."

She held his fierce gaze, even when instinct told her to look away. "Of course it would. The Pantera have gone to a lot of trouble to remain hidden. If you have a rogue psycho attacking women it's going to reveal your presence to the entire world."

Without warning he was standing directly in front of her, his hand cupping her chin as he glared down at her.

"Whoever did this—" With a hiss, Sebastian abruptly jerked his hand from her face, shaking it as if he'd felt the blaze of ruthless need that jolted through her body. Then he went still, something dark and dangerous glowing in his eyes.

Puma.

It wasn't threatening. It was…watchful. Intent. Hungry.

She shivered, and lifted her hand to touch her chin. The skin felt like it'd been scorched.

"What did you do to me?" she husked.

He gave a slow shake of his head. "It wasn't me."

"It had to be you. It was your touch that started this."

"Reny—"

"No."

With a jerky motion she was headed across the foyer and up the stairs, unwilling to acknowledge the brutal arousal that was spreading through her body with every beat of her heart.

God. What the hell was wrong with her?

"Where are you going?"

"The victim's apartment is on the first floor."

Reny walked up the narrow steps, pretending to ignore the image of a stalking panther just inches behind her. He remained silent, but she could sense his tension. The very air sizzled with the heat of his edgy unease.

It was a relief to step out of the stairwell and into the dark hallway, despite the unmistakable stench of urine. Wrinkling her nose, she hurried to knock on the nearest door, forced to wait for a tense minute before it was pulled open to reveal a young woman who clearly was preparing for a night out.

Dressed in nothing more than her bra and panties, the woman pushed her dark hair still damp from the shower out of her eyes and glared at Reny.

"Christ, not you again," she muttered in disgust. "What now?"

"I need to speak with Ms. Handler."

The roommate leaned against the doorjamb, her pretty face already showing signs of her party lifestyle.

"She's not here."

"Do you know when she'll be back?"

"Never."

Reny frowned. "What do you mean, never?"

The woman shrugged. "She packed her bags after the attack and said she had a new place to stay."

Damn. Reny shook her head at her stupidity. She'd already suspected the female victim had received money to lie about her story. She should have known the first thing Koni Handler would do was flee this shithole of an apartment.

"She didn't give you an address?"

"The bitch didn't even leave enough money to cover the utilities. When you find her, tell her I'm going to kick her—" The roommate forgot how to speak as Sebastian suddenly stepped into view. Abruptly straightening from the doorjamb, the woman gave a toss of her hair, arching her back to make sure Sebastian hadn't missed the large tits that were spilling from the tiny lace bra. "Hello there."

Sebastian flashed his killer smile, and Reny had to clench her hands to resist the urge to shove the young woman away and slam the door.

"Did she leave any clothing behind?" he asked.

The woman continued to wave her tits like flags of invitation. "Just a bunch of worthless shit."

"Show me."

Turning, the roommate offered Sebastian a full view of her rounded ass. "I'll show you anything you want, big boy."

Sebastian shot Reny a covert glance, almost as if he sensed the violence that was boiling just below her brittle composure.

"I'll wait here," he murmured. "If you could just get me a shirt?"

The woman didn't bother to hide her irritation at Sebastian's lack of appreciation for her near-naked body, flouncing to snatch a thin top from a sofa that looked remarkably similar to the one in the lobby.

Eww.

"You're not a freak, are you?" she demanded, shoving the shirt in Sebastian's hand.

Sebastian kept his gaze locked on Reny's flushed face. "That's a matter of opinion."

Reny made a choked sound, the arousal pulsing through her reaching a near painful level.

Oh…hell. She had to get away from this man.

Now.

"If you hear from your roommate please give me a call," she muttered, shoving her business card into the woman's hand. She was already headed down the stairs by the time she heard the door slam.

CHAPTER 3

Sebastian gave a low growl at Reny's hasty retreat.

The sensible part of him urged him to bring a halt to the dangerous game.

It was one thing to play along until he could discover if she was an innocent who'd truly been unaware she was Pantera. Or if she was a traitor who was leading him into a trap.

It was another to become lost in the siren song of her mating heat.

A shudder shook his body as his cat savored the spicy arousal drenching the air.

Christ.

It'd been so long since any female had actually been fertile, let alone had broadcast her need with such potency, that it was like a kick in his gut.

Which was all the more reason he should get her to the Healers.

They needed to discover who she was, if her cat had been damaged, and how the hell she was able to project a mating heat when other females had tried and failed for years.

Yeah. That's exactly what he should do.

But as he headed in pursuit of the female, he wasn't reaching for his phone to make the call. His cat had been snared by the intoxicating scent of Reny Smith, and it was on the hunt.

Moving with lethal silence, he jogged down the stairs and out of the building.

Reny drew him on a level that was impossible to resist.

Stalking her through the darkness, he waited until she'd turned the corner before he was moving to stand directly in her path.

"Where are you going?"

"I assume you want the shirt so you can track Ms. Handler." Her words were cool, controlled. But her eyes glowed with a raw need that made his gut twist. "It only makes sense for me to return to the office and start a trace on her finances."

"That can wait." He brushed the back of his fingers over her cheek, groaning at the dewy heat that dampened her skin. His cat roared, not understanding why he was waiting. It didn't care they were on a city street where anyone could see them. It wanted what it wanted and it wanted Reny Smith. "We have something to take care of first."

"What?"

He stepped closer, watching the pulse at the base of her throat flutter out of control. A low growl rumbled in his throat. He wanted to bite that soft flesh. Preferably while he was climaxing, deep inside her, filling her with his seed.

"Come with me."

She licked her dry lips, no doubt seeing the cat

glowing in his eyes. "Actually, I don't feel well."

He lowered his head, nuzzling a line of kisses down her stubborn jaw. "Trust me, I have the only cure."

"How would you know?" she breathed, her body trembling beneath his light caress. "Did you infect me with something?"

He nipped the side of her throat, reveling in her soft gasp of pleasure. "Not exactly."

Her hands landed against his chest, but she didn't push him away. Instead, she gripped his shirt as if her knees were threatening to collapse.

"What is it?" she husked. "What have you done to me?"

His tongue traced the delicate vein that ran the length of her neck. "Not here."

"I'm not going anywhere until you—" She hissed in outrage as he brought an end to the argument by the simple process of grasping her by the waist and tossing her over his shoulder. "Dammit." She pounded her fists against his back, at the same time trying to kick him in his balls. Wildcat. "Put me down."

A feral smile curved Sebastian's lips as he headed toward a far more prosperous neighborhood north of town. He was a Diplomat who'd always preferred to use charm when it came to seducing his women, but he had to admit that the caveman approach did have its appeal.

"You're going to thank me," he assured her, his voice laced with a possession he didn't bother to hide.

"Like hell."

"Trust me," he murmured, moving with a

blinding speed humans could never hope to match.

"Never," she snapped, aiming a kick that would have brought him to his knees if he hadn't turned just enough for her blow to catch his upper thigh.

"Careful, sugar," he purred, his tone oddly pleased. "I intend to use that before the night's over."

She tried to twist her upper body, hoping to reach the gun that was pressing painfully into her side. Not to shoot the aggravating beast. Well, at least not a killing shot. But a slug in his ass would teach him a little respect.

But as if reading her thoughts, he managed to kick up the pace another notch, making her bang and jerk against his back until she feared she was going to be knocked out. She hissed in frustration, her arms wrapping around his waist as the passing buildings became a mere blur.

He continued at the mind-numbing pace as he kept his attention locked on their surroundings, making sure there were no hidden enemies as the streets widened and the houses became mansions hidden behind the veil of Spanish moss.

The quicker he had answers, the better.

For both of them.

At last reaching a white, plantation-style home set well away from the street, Sebastian circled to the back entrance, forced to halt at the steps to place his hand on a scanner. The lock would only open to a Pantera.

With a small swoosh, the heavy metal door swung inward, and Sebastian stepped into the cramped entry, waiting to be electronically scanned by the security system.

A full minute passed before a hidden panel silently slid open, allowing Sebastian to enter the house.

A part of him wished he could lower Reny to her feet and escort her through the large rooms with the molded ceilings and sweeping staircases that captured the airy, graceful beauty of the old South. She deserved to be treated as a treasured guest, not a prisoner. But until he could convince her that he was only trying to help her, he didn't have the luxury.

Regaining her breath, Reny loosened her grip on his waist and gave him another thump on the back.

"What the hell is this place?"

"A safe house for Pantera," he said, using the servants' stairs to reach the second floor.

"Why would you bring me here?"

Sebastian entered the first bedroom. With two long strides he had her dumped on the wide, ivory-canopied bed and had turned to head back out the door.

"Wait here."

"No...don't—"

He shut the door on her furious protest, touching the small lever that would trigger the lock.

The knowledge that he was damaging her trust in him was like a knife through his heart, but he grimly hurried down the stairs and toward the front of the house where he could sense one of his brothers.

Opening the door to what had once been the library, Sebastian stepped into a room that had been stripped of its original furnishings and fitted with the sort of high-tech equipment that could rival the Pentagon.

Pantera might be creatures who'd been born of mist and magic, but they lived in the modern world.

A dark-haired Hunter with whiskey-gold eyes turned away from the line of computer screens he'd been monitoring and rose to his feet.

Lian looked his typical badass self in a pair of faded black jeans and Metallica T-shirt, his long hair pulled into a braid that hung down to his waist.

"Troubles?"

"Here." Sebastian moved forward to shove a long strand of hair into the startled Pantera's hand. "Have this sent to the closest lab and tested."

Lian frowned. "For what?"

"DNA. I want to know what family this comes from."

The Hunter lifted his brows in surprise. "Okay. Anything else?"

"A full background check on Agent Reny Smith, FBI," Sebastian said.

Lian turned to open a desk drawer, pulling out a small baggie to store the hair in. There were several Pantera who worked undercover in the local labs and could expedite the necessary tests.

"It will take at least twenty-four hours for the DNA. I can start the background check now."

Sebastian nodded. "Contact me as soon as you have something."

"You got it."

Confident that he could trust Lian to take care of the search into Reny's past, Sebastian retraced his steps, his body tensing as he reached to push open the door.

God. Damn.

He could physically feel the pulse of Reny's arousal. It was like a fire in his gut.

But slipping into the room, concern was his overriding emotion.

Closing the door, he leaned against it as Reny launched herself at him, her face flushed and tendrils of dark curls that escaped her ponytail pasted to her damp skin.

"You rat bastard," she snarled, slamming her fists against his chest.

Thankful she hadn't shot him the minute he'd opened the door, Sebastian wrapped his arms around her trembling form, pulling her tight against him.

"Shh." He lowered his head, brushing his lips over her temple. The mating heat shouldn't be this intense. It was like a violent force that was pummeling the two of them, instead of the gentle temptation that used to be common among Pantera. "I have you."

"God." She collapsed against his chest, her breath a loud gasp. "What's happening?"

His lips skimmed down her cheek, nuzzling the edge of her mouth. "It's the mating heat."

She pulled back her head to study him in confusion. "You're in heat?"

"Not me." His hand ran a soothing path up and down her back. "You."

"Dammit." Her brows snapped together. "I don't have to listen to this."

"You don't." His fingers cupped the back of her nape, his thumb stroking the pulse that beat at the base of her throat. "But denying the truth isn't going to help either of us. You can feel it, sugar." He peered deep into her gaze, glimpsing the frustrated cat who prowled just below the surface. "Burning deep inside you."

She gave a choked sound. "This has to be a trick."

"No trick." He fiercely held her gaze. The time for games was over. "Your cat has decided to take command."

"I'm not…" She halted to lick her lips, a fear that she could no longer hide tightening her face. "I can't be."

He ignored her ridiculous protests. "You can have your identity crisis later," he assured her. "For now, we need to deal with your discomfort."

"And how do you intend to do that?"

"I can ease you."

She gave a humorless laugh. "Yeah, I bet you can."

His thumb stroked the line of her jaw. "Or I can take you to the Wildlands."

"Why?" she snapped. "So some other puma can ease me?"

A blinding fury raced through him at the mere thought of another man touching this female.

Hell, he'd rip apart anyone stupid enough to get near her.

"Never," he snarled, grimacing as she winced at his feral expression. Sucking in a deep breath, he attempted to calm the beast inside. "Damn. The need shouldn't be this overwhelming," he confessed.

She glared at him, as if it was his fault. "Then why is it?"

"It could be a result of your cat being shackled for too long," he said, his voice a rough growl as he pressed her lower body against his swelling cock. "Or it could be the result of our returning magic. It's been a very long time since we've had a female in heat."

She shook her head, unconsciously curling her fingers into his chest as if she had claws. "Stop saying that."

He bent down until he was pressing his forehead against hers, his nose flaring to capture her deepening musk.

"Tell me what you want, sugar."

"Sanity," she muttered.

No shit. Sebastian could use a hefty dose of that himself.

But it wasn't happening.

Not until the heat was eased.

"Answer me, Reny, before I take the decision out of your hands," he commanded, the edge in his voice warning he was at the point of snapping. "Do we stay, or go to the Wildlands where the Healers might be able discover some pharmaceutical way to lessen your need?"

She trembled, her human mind no doubt urging her to demand to be medically cured of her ache. But it was the cat who was currently in charge, and the too-long suppressed feline wasn't at all confused about what it wanted.

"Stay," she whispered, her eyes glowing. "We stay."

Arousal slammed into him with the force of a cement truck, making it difficult to think as her hand boldly stroked over his chest.

He grasped her wrist, hissing as pleasure poured through him.

"You're sure?"

She answered the strained question by lifting her free hand to continue his torture with bold, searching fingers.

"I don't know what's happening to me, but right now all I want is to wrap myself around you."

Sebastian cursed, his body swiftly threatening to explode. "Be careful what you say to me, sugar. I prefer to be a tender lover, but my cat is ready to devour you."

She didn't look nearly as frightened as she should. "You speak of your cat as a separate being."

"We are one in spirit, but he's far more…primitive. Life is simpler when I'm in my cat form. Life. Death. Hunger." He tangled his fingers into the thick satin of her hair, loosening it from the ponytail so it could spill over her shoulders. His heart skipped a beat as the overhead light shimmered in the fire hidden in the dark satin of her hair. "The thrill of the hunt."

His acute hearing picked up the sudden leap of her heart.

Ah. She liked the idea of being on the prowl.

"Don't think you can hunt me." Leaning forward, she trailed her lips along the curve of his throat. An instinctive provocation that was more Pantera than human. "I'll never be your prey."

Sebastian's fingers loosened on her wrist, his thumb brushing the rapid beat of her pulse. Foolish female. Challenging a Pantera male was a certain way to provoke his most primal instincts.

Strong females were as potent as the finest aphrodisiac to the animal inside him.

Sliding his hand to the front of her neck, his fingers circled her throat, holding her in a gesture of pure possession.

"If I decide you're mine," he murmured softly. "I will hunt you to the end of the earth."

"Is that a threat?" she demanded, her tone distracted as her fingers began to unbutton his shirt.

He gave a low growl, tugging her tight against his hard body.

"It's a promise, sugar," he rasped, his senses inflamed to the point of pain.

"This is madness." She pulled open his shirt, trailing her tongue down the bronzed skin she'd just revealed. "Complete lunacy."

His soft groan rumbled in his chest as he moved to cup her ass, compulsively pressing her to his rock hard cock.

"You won't get an argument from me," he muttered, for the first time fully appreciating the power of the mating heat.

Her hunger was a savage ache that clenched his body, the temptation of her spicy scent drowning him in need.

His cock throbbed in concert with every beat of her heart.

"Have you ever done this?"

He gave a startled laugh. "Had sex?"

She arched back to meet his searching gaze, an unexpected hint of vulnerability in her eyes.

"Have you been with many females in my…condition?"

Unable to resist the sight of that slender neck arched in open invitation, Sebastian lowered his head.

"No," he murmured, his voice a husky growl. "Never."

She gave a low groan as his tongue ran a searing path along the line of her throat.

"Then how do you know this will put an end to it?" Her fingers dug into his upper arms, as if her knees had suddenly become too weak to support her.

He nipped her earlobe, wryly acknowledging that the mating heat was only an excuse to give in to his desire.

He would have done everything in his power to get her in the nearest bed without the heat driving him.

"There's only one way to find out."

Before she could even guess his intention, Sebastian was easing her out of her jacket and unbuckling her holster to set aside her gun before swiftly dealing with the white cotton shirt. Then, reaching the end of his patience, he rid her of the lacy white bra with one sharp tug.

Sebastian made a sound of appreciation, his hands moving to cup her breasts with a reverent care.

Damn. He'd suspected she'd be beautiful beneath all that starch, but she was…perfect.

His thumbs teased the pink tips of her nipples, rumbling in pleasure as they hardened with excitement.

"Do you like that?" he demanded.

"Yes," she whispered.

His head lowered, his lips closing over the sensitive nipple. "And this?"

Her head dropped back, a low purr vibrating in her chest.

"Oh...hell, yes."

Softly chuckling at her eager response, Sebastian leashed his urge to pounce. Falling on her like a rabid puma probably wasn't the best idea. Not for their first time.

Continuing to tease her nipple with his tongue, Sebastian deftly slid down the zipper of her slacks, eager to feel her naked body pressed against his. When there was no protest from Reny, he slowly began to peel them downward, lowering himself to his knees as he efficiently tugged off her sensible shoes before he finished stripping her.

Then, still kneeling, he allowed himself to drink in her beauty.

She was long and slender, but had the firm muscles of a Pantera rippling beneath her smooth skin.

Excitement scorched through him as his attention lingered on the tiny triangle of silk that was all that covered her. Well...it didn't actually *cover* much.

Who would have suspected that beneath all that starch Reny Smith, FBI agent, was a woman who wore a bright red thong?

His cat snarled, urging him to rethink that whole 'no pouncing' decision.

Once again, however, he restrained his primitive impulse.

Instead, he skimmed his lips up the flat plane of her stomach, the valley between her breasts, at last halting at the pulse that beat wildly at the base of her neck.

She made a sound of impatience, her lips parting willingly as he at last claimed her mouth in a kiss of sheer possession.

"Sebastian," she moaned.

"If you have any intention of changing your mind, it'd better be quick, sugar," he warned. "My control is about to snap."

"Let it snap," she whispered against his lips.

"Last chance," he offered, his hands clenching the gentle swell of her hips.

He knew once he had a taste of her it would not be enough.

Because this is way more than the mating heat.
This woman belongs in my arms.

The unnerving words seared through his mind before he could halt them.

"My last chance ended when I arrived in New Orleans," she retorted, shivering as his tongue swiped between her lips in a very feline gesture. "I should never have left New York."

"I would have found you, Reny Smith," he said, grasping her hand to gently place it against his pulsing arousal. "This moment was fated from the day we were born."

She held his gaze as her fingers traced his hard cock that strained against his zipper, her eyes glowing with the power of her cat.

Hunger clawed deep within him. Okay, maybe no pouncing, but a raw, pagan night of sex was becoming far more likely.

As if deliberately attempting to drive Sebastian out of his mind, Reny tugged down the zipper of his slacks, releasing the heavy thrust of his erection.

"And I've never been so damned happy with destiny in my entire life," Sebastian managed to croak, shuddering at the hot surge of pleasure.

Heat spiked the air as she lightly skimmed her fingers down his thick length.

"I don't believe in that mumbo-jumbo," she muttered.

"You should. Fate brought you to me," he growled, his hands tightening on her hips as he sought to leash his eager cat.

"No, I control my own life," she stubbornly insisted, her hand moving steadily lower.

"Reny…" He muttered a curse, his eyes clenching shut. How the hell was he supposed to argue when he was one stroke away from a climax? "Are you deliberately trying to torture me?"

She discovered his tender sack and lightly squeezed. "Would I do that?"

"Yes," he choked, grasping her wrist to halt the exquisite torment. "No more."

"Why not?"

Forcing his eyes open, he met the glowing moss green eyes. "Because just your touch is about to make me explode."

The spicy scent of her arousal spiked at his blunt words. "And that's a bad thing?"

"Not bad," he husked. "But I want to be buried deep inside you when I come."

She shivered, responding to the stark need in his

voice. "Then what are you waiting for?"

Good question.

Granted, he wasn't like many of his people. He was calm, calculated. Capable of considering a situation from multiple viewpoints.

That's what made him such a successful Diplomat. He didn't allow his instincts to rule him.

But now…

Now he wanted to plunge into the incandescent pleasure that was heating his blood to a fever pitch. He wanted to forget the danger that continued to threaten the Wildlands. And the knowledge that Raphael was depending on him to bring an end to the humans' mounting fear.

He just wanted to become lost in his hunger for a woman who was stirring emotions that should have terrified the hell out of him.

With a slow, sensuous gesture, Sebastian loosened his grip on her wrist at the same moment he captured her lips with a blazing kiss. She opened her mouth to invite the invasion of his tongue, her hand moving down his cock with a stroke that made his back arch in pure bliss.

Gliding his lips over the flushed skin of her cheeks, he discovered the sensitive spot just below her ear. She shivered in response, her heart pounding so loudly that Sebastian didn't need to be Pantera to hear it.

He used her soft sighs to guide his growingly insistent caresses, focused on her pleasure even as his hips began to pump in rhythm with her forceful strokes.

Oh…hell.

This wasn't how he expected this to play out, but it felt so fucking good.

Reaching that surprising thong, Sebastian ripped it away with one firm tug. Screw subtle.

He had one goal in mind, and nothing was allowed to stand in his way.

Skimming his hand over the curve of her thigh, Sebastian gently urged her legs to part, giving his fingers access to her most tender flesh.

A low growl rumbled in his throat as he parted her folds to discover that she was already damp and eager for his touch.

"Christ," she muttered, her hand unwittingly clenching on his cock as he pressed a finger into her body.

Not that he protested. Hell, no. He was all about muttering soft words of encouragement as he caressed her with a growing urgency.

His cat growled in frustration, wanting to possess the female in a far more intimate way, but Sebastian ignored the burning need to press her against the wall and fuck her until she screamed in pleasure.

Reny wasn't used to having sex with a Pantera male.

He needed to blunt the savage edge of his need.

Besides, the blissful pressure clenching his lower body was swiftly reaching the point of no return. He was fiercely determined to ensure her pleasure before claiming his own.

Lowering his head, Sebastian sucked the tip of her nipple in his mouth, using his teeth to tease her as his finger slid in and out of her slick channel. She whimpered softly, her hand stroking him with greater urgency.

He could sense that she was close.

Her spicy heat filled the room, intoxicating his senses.

Her breath locked in her throat, her back arching. Then, with a soft cry, she shuddered in completion, her last, insistent tug of his erection causing him to cry out as his climax slammed through him and the world shattered in pleasure.

Wrapping her in his arms, Sebastian had to smile.

Reny was wrong.

This had to be fate.

Nothing less than divine intervention could have brought this exquisite, mysterious female into his arms.

CHAPTER 4

Pleasure scalded through Reny, making her knees weak as she clung to the man who'd just given her the most shattering climax of her life.

Good. God.

That was...

Her fuzzy mind struggled to form the words that would capture the spasms of pleasure that continued to clench her body.

It didn't make sense.

Sebastian was barely more than a stranger. Hell, they hadn't even had full intercourse.

She wanted to blame the blinding enjoyment on the weird-ass mating heat.

Any man would do while she was being forced into sex by a chemical-induced frenzy.

Problem was...she knew that wasn't true.

Yes, she'd been driven by a hunger she'd never felt before. At least, not that she could remember. And her logical mind would never have allowed her to get up close and personal with a man she'd just met if it wasn't for the lust that had thundered through her body.

But, there was no way that she'd have given in to

her desire if she hadn't been attracted to Sebastian on a deep, primal level. And she certainly wouldn't still be aching to push him onto the nearby bed and impale herself on the hard length of his cock.

Almost as if able to read her thoughts, Sebastian lowered his head to nuzzle his face against her cheek in a very feline gesture.

She shivered. How could such a simple caress be so amazingly erotic?

"Better?" he murmured against her ear.

She gave a small nod, still trying to catch her breath. "It's not as…" She hesitated, allowing herself to consider the faint buzz of arousal that continued to race through her. It was there…waiting…but it was no longer a clawing, almost painful desire. As if Sebastian's touch had reassured the strange hunger that her needs were going to be met. How crazy was that? "Persistent," she at last muttered.

His lips touched her temple before following her hairline to trace the shell of her ear. "Good."

She sucked in a deep breath, discovering the exotic musk of his skin was as enticing as his hard, chiseled body and the soft caress of his fingers as they trailed up and down her back.

"Good?"

"When I take you, we'll both know that it's because you want to."

She pulled back to meet his eyes that still glowed with blatant lust. "You're so certain I want you?"

"Yes."

"Arrogant."

He flashed a smile filled with sinful promise as he

released her to shrug out of his shirt. Reny nearly choked as she caught her first full glimpse of Sebastian's bare chest.

He was delectable.

Her fingers itched to explore the broad expanse of bronzed skin, lingering on the six-pack before lowering to the cock that was rising and thickening at her appreciative glance.

Or maybe she'd use her tongue, she abruptly decided, giving up any pretense that she wasn't eager to finish what they'd started.

It wasn't like he didn't sense her reaction to his striptease.

Just as she could feel the pulse of his mounting desire beating against her.

Heat prickled over her skin, her mouth going dry as he kicked off the Italian leather shoes and shoved down the black slacks.

Oh, man. He looked like he'd been sculpted by an artist.

The urge to touch him was too much to resist. Reaching out, she was caught off guard when Sebastian shackled her wrist in a strong grip.

"No," he growled, the cat so close to the surface that Reny would swear she could *sense* it.

She lifted her brows in surprise. "You don't like my touch?"

"Too much," he confessed with blunt honesty, tugging her against his naked body. Reny swallowed a startled gasp at the skin to skin contact. It felt like she was being branded. Claimed in a way she didn't fully grasp. Sebastian gave a low growl of approval, his smile smug. "The last time I let you to take control, allowing you to take what you needed from me. It's my turn."

His dominance was like a physical push against her. It should have annoyed the hell out of her.

Reny was far too independent to put up with a man who treated her as anything less than an equal.

So why was the feel of his raw, predatory strength sending tiny tremors of anticipation through her body?

Annoyed by her traitorous response, she narrowed her gaze.

"I like to be in control."

His hands skimmed up her back to tangle his fingers in her hair, tilting her head back so he could have full access to the vulnerable length of her neck.

"Yeah, I noticed." His lips traced a path of havoc along her jaw, before nibbling down the curve of her throat. "But you're going to like my way better."

Like?

She was freaking *loving* it.

"Oh, really?" she forced herself to mutter, even though she wasn't fooling anyone.

He chuckled, swiping a rough tongue over the sensitive spot between her neck and shoulder.

"Sugar, I'm going to make you scream."

"You can try."

"Ah, a challenge," he whispered, as his hands slid over her shoulders and toward her aching breasts. "I can be very persuasive when I'm motivated."

She made a choked sound as his thumbs brushed over her straining nipples. Why had she never noticed how sensitive they were? Probably because she'd never been touched by Sebastian.

Just having him near was enough to make her entire body sizzle with eagerness.

The reluctant acknowledgement had barely formed when it was buried beneath an avalanche of pleasure as his mouth skated over the curve of her breast. Reaching his destination, his lips closed over the tip so his tongue could tease her with merciless skill.

"Not fair," she muttered, her fingers shoving into the tawny silk of his hair.

He turned his head to torment her other breast.

"I never play fair," he warned her, lifting his head to meet her heated gaze. "I play to win."

With a motion too swift for Reny to anticipate, Sebastian swept her off her feet and tossed her into the center of the bed, her arms and legs splayed wide.

"Hey."

"We're doing things my way this time, remember?" he demanded, covering her with the welcome weight of his body.

She lifted her hands, intending to hold him off so she could tell him exactly what she thought of his arrogance. Only her hands were no longer connected to her brain. Rather than pushing against the hard planes of his chest, her fingers were lingering on a small tattoo of a crouching puma that was barely noticeable against the bronzed skin of his chest.

"I never agreed," she said, her voice a husky rasp.

Lowering his head, Sebastian nibbled at the corner of her mouth. "Do you need me to convince you?"

A harsh shudder shook her body. Oh, yeah. She was ready and willing to be convinced.

Somewhere in the back of her mind she knew that this was a brief moment of madness, first brought on by the strange sexual compulsion and now by her purely feminine desire.

And perhaps the need to forget the world for just a little while.

Beyond the closed door was her duty to finish the job that had brought her to New Orleans. And impressing her bosses to ensure her promotion.

And, oh yeah, somehow processing the suspicion that she wasn't entirely human.

Sometimes a woman needed a few hours of fantasy to make her reality more bearable.

And Sebastian was the perfect fantasy.

As if sensing her capitulation, Sebastian growled low in his throat, his hands moving with a possessive confidence over her naked body.

"Spice and musk," he muttered, his tongue outlining her lips. "I need a taste."

Reny gave a small squeak as one roaming hand slid between her thighs to stroke through her wet pussy.

"Do you bite?" she asked, breathless.

"Absolutely." He held her gaze as he dipped his finger into her thickening cream. "But only if you beg nicely."

Reny dug her heels into the black silk sheets as she arched her hips upward.

"As if…" She forgot how to speak as his finger began sliding in and out of her. "Oh."

His lips brushed over her cheek, then down the line of her jaw. "Let yourself go, Agent Reny Smith." He pressed a kiss to the pulse racing at the base of her throat. "Just." His mouth trailed down her collarbone. "Let." He covered the aching tip of her breast. "Go."

Oh, hell. Maybe he was going to make her scream. Her entire body was going up in flames.

Fisting her fingers in his thick hair, she instinctively wrapped her legs around his hips.

"Stop giving me orders and do this thing."

Pulling back, he regarded her with a lift of his brows. "Do this thing?"

"You heard me."

"Hmm." His smile was mysterious. "I wonder if your cat is as demanding as you are."

She deliberately rubbed herself against the granite-hard length of his erection, not ready to consider what sort of animal lurked inside her. "Does it matter?"

The yellow in his eyes glowed until they appeared incandescent in the dim light.

Bracing himself on his elbow, he altered his position until the tip of his cock pressed against her entrance. "You are going to be all kinds of trouble, sugar."

She sucked in a breath of anticipation, her pussy parting in welcome as he surged deep inside her with a slow, relentless thrust.

Moving her hands, Reny clutched at Sebastian's shoulders, her nails digging into his skin. Holy crap. He was huge. Deliciously, heart-stoppingly huge. She groaned. There wasn't pain. Despite Sebastian's considerable size, her body eagerly accommodated his entry. But there was a sensual sense of fullness, and a startling intimacy that she hadn't been expecting.

In this moment she felt utterly bonded to Sebastian. Bonded in a way that seemed far more poignant than two bodies simply having sex.

It was...

No. She slammed a mental door on the dangerous thoughts. She couldn't afford for this to be more than a meaningless, transitory coupling.

"Reny," he whispered close to her ear. "Are you okay?"

"Yes," she muttered, burying her face in the curve of his neck. "Don't stop."

"Christ, I couldn't stop if you put a gun to my head," he muttered, withdrawing from her body before pushing back in with a growing urgency. "I've never felt anything more perfect."

He was right.

It was perfect.

The heat and weight of his body as he pressed her deep into the mattress. The intoxicating musk that filled her senses. The beauty of his bronzed face, tight with the strain of tempering his hunger.

But before she could agree, he was once again pulling out and thrusting forward with a rhythm that stole her breath. Yes. Oh, yes. This was what her body had longed for in the depths of the night. This was what she needed.

Savoring the savage pleasure of his possession, Reny raked her nails down his back, delighted by the growl that reverberated in his chest. She dug her nails deeper, rewarded as he angled her head so he could sink his teeth into the vulnerable flesh of her neck.

He did bite.

His hips rocked faster, his hands tilting her upward to meet his deep, steady thrusts.

"Sebastian…please," she implored, her body coiled so tightly she felt as if she might shatter.

"I told you to let go." Dipping his head downward, he teased her aching nipple with his lips, pumping with a brutal pace as she wrapped her legs around his waist.

Reny's breath rasped in the silent air, her focus locked onto the point where Sebastian's body slammed in and out of her.

She was so close. So divinely close.

And then…pow.

It happened.

With one last surge he tumbled her over the edge, galvanizing her into an orgasm that exploded with blissful force. Her scream of pleasure reverberated through the room, her body shuddering with bliss as he continued to pump into her until he stiffened with his own release, his back arching beneath the force of his climax.

Wrenching open her eyes, she regarded him in horror.

Dammit. He'd made her scream.

Meeting her gaze, he allowed a smug smile to curve his lips. "Gotcha."

CHAPTER 5

Sebastian purred, basking in the heat of Reny's body entwined with his own.

Mmm. He was satisfied on a level that went way beyond a good orgasm.

Sated lust was a good thing.

Hell, it was a great thing.

But this sense of…bone-deep rightness…it made him feel as if he'd just won the fucking lottery.

He was in trouble.

The kind of trouble that led a male Pantera into mating for life.

But he didn't care.

Fate had given him this female and there was no way in hell he was letting her go.

Nuzzling his lips against her temple, Sebastian trailed his fingers over her toned abs, relishing the spicy scent that fully captured this complicated woman.

Sassy, strong, unpredictable.

"That was—" His words were cut short when Reny pressed her fingers to his lips.

"No."

He arched a brow. "No?"

"I don't want to dissect what happened between us."

Propping himself on his elbow, he carefully studied her wary expression.

Her dark hair was spread across the pillows, hidden streaks of red shimmering like fire in the muted overhead light. Her face was still flushed from their combustible passion. And her slender body was perfectly formed to curve against him.

Her beauty was like an incandescent flame that drew him like a moth.

But it was the stubborn set of her jaw that captured his attention.

Reny Smith might have given her body with a generosity that had stolen his heart, but it was obvious her mind refused to accept the inevitable bond that was forming between them.

He smiled wryly. He didn't know whether to be annoyed with her stubborn resistance, or excited by the thought of continuing the chase.

It would make her eventual surrender all the sweeter.

Leaning down, he nipped the tip of her nose. "Are you always so romantic with your lovers?"

"I'm practical," she said in defensive tones. "I've had to be."

"Why?"

"When you have your past stolen from you by amnesia you swiftly discover the world isn't a place for fairy tales."

Amnesia...hell, that would explain so much.

"You were in an accident?"

"There was some sort of trauma." Old sorrow

darkened her moss green eyes. "I was found hidden in the back of a semi-truck. I had wounds on my wrists and ankles that proved I'd been bound for several days, if not weeks. Maybe even longer. The doctors speculated that I'd been held by a psychopath and my mind had blocked out the memories of my torture."

Sebastian barely dared to breathe as fury exploded through him. This sweet, fragile woman had been abused by a madman?

It was no wonder she'd been forced to build walls in her mind. Not only to deal with the horror of her captivity, but to contain the cat inside her that had never been allowed to fully bond with her.

Christ, she had to be one of the strongest people he'd ever met to not only survive, but to have built a new life for herself.

His fingers gently stroked her cheek, the need to ease her pain a physical necessity.

"How did you join the FBI?"

She turned in to his light caress, unconsciously seeking the comfort of his touch. "The cops who found me took me under their wing when it became obvious I wasn't going to be able to find my family." A tremor raced through her body. No doubt she'd tormented herself over the years with the image of how her parents must have been frantic in their search for their missing daughter. "They encouraged me to apply to Quantico."

Sebastian frowned. How was it possible that he hadn't heard of a missing Pantera female?

Her parents would have come to the Wildlands for assistance in searching for her

Unless they were dead.

Which meant the bastard holding her might not have been a random psycho.

"Did they find the man responsible for holding you?" he murmured.

She shook her head. "They searched, but they couldn't even be entirely certain that's what happened to me."

"Perhaps they were looking in the wrong place."

"What do you mean?"

He absently smoothed a strand of hair behind her ear. "The Pantera have enemies."

Her lips parted, but before she could interrogate him, there was a series of beeps from across the room.

"That's the office," she muttered, wriggling out of his arms to hop out of bed.

Sebastian gave a low growl of protest, but he couldn't deny an appreciation of watching her naked ass as she moved to pick up her jacket and pull out the ringing phone.

It was a very fine ass, he acknowledged, wishing he'd done more exploring of the lush temptation.

Next time…

His indulgent fantasies of the various ways he intended to savor Reny were interrupted as he watched her expression become grim as she listened to the caller.

Instantly, he was off the bed and pulling on his clothes. Their all-too-brief moment of privacy was over.

It was time to rejoin the world.

"What happened?" he demanded as soon as she ended the call.

She dressed with a brisk efficiency. "There was another mauling."

"Damn." Sebastian tucked his shirt in his pants and smoothed back his hair. "I need to talk to the victim."

"You can't."

"Why not?" His brows snapped together as he watched her slip on her sensible leather shoes and tug her hair into a tight ponytail.

Once again she was the starchy Agent Smith.

His cat growled in disapproval.

She lifted her head to meet his annoyed glare. "She's at the morgue."

Oh…hell.

Sebastian's gut twisted with regret. He'd known it was only a matter of time before their enemies took their attacks to the next level, but he'd hoped he would be able to expose them before they actually killed someone.

"Do you know where they found the body?"

Reny grimaced. "It was propped next to the dumpster at the police station."

"Bold bastards." Sebastian pulled out his phone and texted the info to Raphael. The Wildlands needed to be prepared in case the humans decided to retaliate. "They wanted to make sure it was found."

"Yes."

Sebastian slid the phone back into his pocket. "We need to find the first victim."

"I agree."

With an obvious refusal to glance toward the bed that was a visual display of their recent passion, she headed to pull open the door.

Before she could step out of the room, however, he captured her from behind. Wrapping his arm around her waist, he whispered directly in her ear.

"You know this isn't finished."

She held herself stiffly, but there was no missing the rapid beat of her heart.

"Don't push your luck, cat," she warned.

He traced the curve of her ear with his tongue. "Sugar, I'm going to push until I hear you scream again." He planted a kiss in the hollow beneath her jaw. "And again." He gently sank his teeth into the tender flesh between her neck and shoulder, chuckling as she groaned in startled pleasure. "And—"

Giving a small hiss, Reny broke out of his hold, turning to meet his smoldering gaze.

"Are all Pantera so cocky?"

An unexpected, shockingly violent tidal wave of territorial possession surged through him. "I'm the only Pantera you need to worry about." There was a hint of warning in his voice. "Period."

Her eyes widened, but perhaps sensing the danger of poking his cat when it was anxious to pounce, she deliberately stepped into the hall.

"Where do we start?" she asked.

Sebastian squashed the urge to scoop her in his arms and carry her back to bed. His growingly urgent need to bond with Reny Smith would have to wait until they'd brought a halt to the bastards who were attacking defenseless women.

"Back at the apartment," he said, hoping Koni Handler had the information he needed to start his hunt. "I need to pick up the female's scent."

"Makes sense," she agreed, briskly heading down the stairs.

Sebastian prowled at her side. "You should return to your office and start running her financials."

She pulled out her phone and began typing in a message. "I can have one of the techs take care of it."

They moved down the stairs and toward the back of the house. "Then you can go have dinner."

"I already ate." She sent him a suspicious glare. "Why are you trying to get rid of me?"

"We don't know what's out there hunting women," he said.

A dangerous heat sparked in her eyes. "Exactly. It's my job to find out."

He was a Diplomat. He knew that tone.

It meant, 'You've just pissed on my last nerve. Now back off.'

But he was also a Pantera male who possessed an instinctive need to protect his female.

"You don't understand the danger."

Heat sizzled through the air, the power of her cat glowing in her eyes.

"Don't you dare treat me like a helpless little woman." She stepped forward, poking her finger into the middle of his chest. "This is my case." Another poke, this one hard enough to hurt. "If you don't want to be my partner then return to the Wildlands and send someone else."

Oh, hell. She was a born Hunter. He could read it in her fierce need to be out tracking down their enemies. It was no wonder that she'd chosen to go into law enforcement.

Sebastian smothered a wry smile.

She was going to make his life…interesting.

"Come on," he said.

***

Reny was prepared to remain on her personal soapbox. There was nothing she hated more than being treated as if she couldn't be good at her job because she had a uterus instead of a penis.

But the moment they'd returned to the desolate neighborhood where Koni Handler had lived, Sebastian wisely resisted any urge to try and prevent her from remaining at his side as he focused on following the scent.

A scent that teased at Reny's nose even while she slammed the door on acknowledging her abilities.

It was a trick she'd developed when she was in the hospital and realized how different she was from the other patients.

How else could she stay sane?

They'd traveled three blocks when Sebastian came to a sudden halt, his expression grim as he glanced around the corner that was bathed in the gaudy lights from a nearby bar.

"Why are you stopping?" she demanded.

"She must have gotten into a vehicle." He gave a frustrated growl. "Dammit."

"Then we do it the human way," Reny murmured, her trained gaze instantly searching near the doorway of the bar. She was rewarded by the sight of a small red light. "There." She pointed toward the surveillance camera.

He arched a brow, looking impossibly gorgeous despite his ruffled hair and the hint of tawny whiskers that shadowed his jaw.

"Good call. Can you get us access?"

Something eased in her chest at his ready willingness to accept her help.

Maybe he wasn't a complete jackass.

With a smug smile she pulled her badge from the inner pocket of her jacket and headed across the street.

Entering the narrow bar with a dozen worn tables scattered over a wood floor, Reny took a direct path toward the back of the room where a large, grizzled man was tending bar. A few of the drunken patrons gave her a lingering look before paling in fear as they caught sight of the predatory male who walked a half step behind her.

Less than ten minutes later they were in a cramped office that smelled of scotch and cheap cologne, skimming through fuzzy images that flashed across the computer screen.

"There she is," Reny said, halting the video as she recognized Koni Handler stepping into a white van with an emblem painted on its side of a spread-winged raven flying across a full moon.

"Shit." Sebastian leaned over her shoulder, his expression grim. "Can you enlarge it?"

She zoomed in on the blurred image of the driver. "Do you recognize him?"

The heat from his body pumped through the room. "Unfortunately."

Her breath caught in her throat as she glanced up to meet his bloodthirsty gaze. "Is he Pantera?"

"No," he instantly denied. "But I think I know how to find him."

She rose to her feet, heading out of the office. "We'll take my car."

"Yes, ma'am," he teased, allowing her to lead them out of the bar and down the street.

She waited until they were in her car and Sebastian had punched in the GPS coordinates that had them heading east before she asked the obvious question.

"How do you know the driver?"

There was another blast of heat, revealing that beneath Sebastian's façade of calm focus was a smoldering fury.

"We discovered that he's a disciple for our enemy."

"Disciple?" She sent him a puzzled glance. "That's a strange term."

"They worship the goddess who's determined to destroy us."

She searched his tense profile, looking for some indication he was screwing with her.

"A goddess?"

"Yes." His fingers tapped on his knee, clearly impatient to get to where they were going. "Which means this might be even worse than we originally anticipated."

Shit. He was serious.

"What goddess?" she demanded, wondering if the night could get any more bizarre. "And why does she want to destroy you?"

"I promise to explain it as soon as we find our

missing victim," he said, his tone distracted.

Reny grimaced, not in the mood to insist on answers.

She was still trying to accept the thought that she might be a Pantera.

She didn't want to add in a mysterious goddess who might or might not want to destroy her.

They traveled in silence as Reny followed the GPS directions to the edge of town. At last, she turned into what looked like an abandoned industrial complex.

"Pull over there." Sebastian pointed toward a stack of pylons. She parked the car and shut off the engine, already prepared when he turned to send her a worried glance. "Reny."

"Don't." She pointed a warning finger into his face. "Start."

With a roll of his eyes, he shoved open the door and climbed out of the car. Reny pulled her gun from the holster before following him through the thick shadows toward a three-story brick building at the edge of the complex.

Expecting him to head directly for the loading doors that stood open, Reny was caught off guard when he took a wide path around the far edge of the building.

"Where are we going?" she demanded, keeping her voice pitched low so it wouldn't carry.

"There could be Pantera," he explained. "We need to stay downwind."

She jumped over a pile of coiled steel cable that was nearly hidden by the patches of weeds.

Damn. She was going to end up with a broken neck if she wasn't careful.

"I thought you said a Pantera couldn't be involved," she said.

His pace never slowed. "I said a Pantera couldn't shift away from the Wildlands, not that we haven't discovered traitors among our people."

"Great," she muttered. "Any other surprises you want to spring on me?"

He glanced over his shoulder with a grin that made her blood heat. "Not while you're clothed."

She cursed at the instant lust that raced through her body. "Arrogant cat."

CHAPTER 6

Sebastian reluctantly led Reny toward the narrow door at the end of the abandoned warehouse, knowing it would be a waste of breath to try and convince her to wait in the car.

Besides, he couldn't change her nature.

Reny Smith was a born warrior. To try and make her less would break something deep inside her.

Not that it wasn't going to make him crazy to have her charging into danger.

With one sharp tug, Sebastian had the padlock broken and was pushing open the door. Then, with a silence that no human could hope to achieve, he was sliding through the vast room that had once been filled with crates of animal pelts. The lingering odor might have masked the presence of the four humans if they hadn't been bonded to Shakpi. The sour stench that clung to her disciples couldn't be missed.

Halting in the shadows, Sebastian studied the humans who remained oblivious to his presence.

There was a young woman he assumed was Koni Handler. She was tied to a chair, her head bent down so her hair fell forward to hide her face, although he could hear her soft sobs from across the room.

Several feet away was an older woman with several bracelets on her scrawny arms, dressed in a brightly patterned dress. Her silver hair was pulled into a knot at the back of her head and she was currently giving two human males the evil eye.

Sebastian growled deep in his throat. There was a redheaded male with a scar that twisted one side of his face, but it was the man with lanky black hair and a rat face that Sebastian had recognized from the video surveillance.

Derek.

The bastard who'd been pretending to be an ally to the Pantera when all along he was working for their enemies.

On the plus side, it was Derek's stupidity that had allowed the Geeks to track his movements from the voodoo shop where he'd been spying on Isi to this warehouse. Which was how Sebastian knew exactly where to locate him.

Clearly not any more impressed with the thug's intelligence than Sebastian was, the older woman pointed her finger toward the bound woman, the heavy bracelets that circled her arms giving a loud rattle.

"You were told to kill her and dump the body."

"We did with the ugly one," the redhead muttered, hunching his shoulders. "This one we want to play with first."

"Idiots." The woman that he suspected was Lady Cerise stepped forward to slap the man on the side of his head. "My informant just called to warn me that a Pantera is in town working with the FBI. Do you want to lead them to us?"

Sebastian silently cursed, making a mental note to track down the informant. He wouldn't tolerate traitors.

"They have no way of finding this place," Derek boasted.

"You know nothing," Lady Cerise snapped. "It's easy to be a bully when you're dealing with the dregs of humanity. The Pantera will eat you alive." She allowed a dramatic pause. "Literally."

"I'm not scared," Derek muttered, ruining his cocky boast when he sent a nervous glance toward the shadows that shrouded the warehouse.

Did he sense they were near? Sebastian hoped so.

He wanted him afraid. To feel hunted.

"Because you're stupid." Lady Cerise pointed out the obvious. "Now get rid of her."

The redhead folded his arms over his chest. "You ain't in charge."

There was a shocked silence.

"What did you say?" the older woman at last rasped.

"Our goddess, Shakpi, has returned," the man said. "She's in charge now."

Sebastian covered Reny's mouth with lightning speed, easily sensing her shock at the revelation that the goddess he'd mentioned earlier was actually walking the earth. He'd hoped to avoid sharing that little tidbit of info. At least until she'd managed to process the other shocks she'd had to endure over the past few hours.

Across the cavernous room, Derek gave a nervous laugh. "Even if she does look like a middle-aged Indian dude."

"No shit," the redhead agreed with a chuckle.

Not amused, Lady Cerise deliberately grasped a small satin bag she had tied around her neck.

"You will do as I say or I will place a curse on you that will cause a body part to fall off each and every day. Starting with your very small dicks." The woman offered an evil smile. "Do you understand?"

The two men shuddered at the threat. "Fine."

Sebastian was distracted as Reny pressed against him to whisper directly in his ear. "I have to do something."

He wisely bit back his instinctive refusal, reminding himself that Reny would never forgive him if he tried to cage her.

Besides, he was going to need her if they were to get the female out alive.

Assuring himself that he'd soon have her back in the Wildlands where she would be safe, he turned to meet her steady gaze.

"I'll distract them," he murmured softly. "You circle around and get the girl." Something that might have been relief darkened her eyes, as if she'd been dreading his refusal to accept her help. Of course, he couldn't completely resist giving out at least one warning. "Don't take any unnecessary risks."

Narrowing her gaze, she abruptly framed his face in her hands and glared at his startled expression.

"You."

"Yes?"

"Be careful."

He blinked in surprise, having expected a lecture, not a warning. Warmth spread through his heart as she brushed her lips across his with a kiss that promised far more wicked pleasures to come.

"Careful is my middle name."

She gave a shake of her head. "I'm fairly certain your middle name is Aggravating Bastard."

He stole another kiss before straightening and nodding his head toward the west wall. "Take the female out the side door and call for backup."

With a smooth efficiency, Reny was moving along the edge of the room, her gun held in a professional grip.

Good girl, he silently approved, waiting until she was approaching the bound female before he stalked forward, using the sheer power of his presence to capture the villains' attention.

Even humans could sense when there was a predator in their midst.

Halting a few feet away, he folded his arms over his chest.

"You should listen to…" He glanced toward the older woman. "Lady Cerise, I presume?"

The redhead clenched his hands, deliberately flexing his muscles. As if Sebastian would be impressed. Twit.

"Who the hell are you?" he blustered.

"I could say I'm your worst nightmare but that would be so clichéd." His smile was mocking. "Oh, the hell with it. I'm your worst nightmare."

Out of the corner of his eye, Sebastian watched as Reny silently crept forward and began working on the ropes that held the nearly unconscious female.

Confident she could complete her mission,

Sebastian briefly watched Lady Cerise scuttle away, accepting he'd have to track her down later before he returned his attention to the redhead who was taking a step forward.

"Careful, Van," Derek warned. "He's one of those fucking animals."

Van turned his head to spit on the ground, revealing the image of a raven that had been branded on his neck. The Mark of Shakpi.

"I've had my rabies shots," he assured his friend, acting all badass with the knowledge they had Sebastian outnumbered.

Sebastian arched a brow. "Wanna play, tough guy?"

"Play with this." Pulling a gun from a holster at his lower back, Van squeezed the trigger.

Sebastian easily dodged the bullet and stalked forward.

"Shit, do something," the man rasped, emptying his magazine in an attempt to halt Sebastian's relentless approach.

"Like it's doing you any good?" Derek muttered, abruptly retreating toward a nearby storage room.

"Where are you going?" Van demanded as his companion fled, finally realizing that Lady Cerise had disappeared at the first sight of Sebastian. "Goddamn cowards."

Sebastian allowed his smile to widen, breathing deeply of the man's rising terror. These bastards had not only attacked helpless females, but they were deliberately trying to create trouble between Pantera and humans.

They deserved to be punished.

Still he forced himself to wait before he attacked the fool. Reny was still urging the stumbling female across the floor. Once he was sure she was safely out of the building, he would—

Concentrating on Reny, Sebastian failed to notice Derek stepping back out of the storage room with a small gun in his hand. Not that he would be worried even if he had.

A bullet would hurt like a bitch, but it couldn't kill a Pantera.

But it wasn't a bullet that he felt stab into his neck.

Instead, it was a tiny dart.

Baffled by the ridiculous weapon, Sebastian reached up to pluck the dart from his neck, instantly recognizing the toxic potion that the Pantera had recently discovered being used by Shakpi's disciples.

A numbing sensation spread through his body with terrifying swiftness, cutting off his connection to his cat.

Shit. He couldn't shift when he was away from the Wildlands, but his strength and superior senses were directly connected to the power of his animal.

Turning to charge the bastard, he felt his knees threaten to give away as the toxin pumped through his bloodstream.

"Damn."

His last thought was relief that Reny was headed away from the warehouse, before Derek slammed a two-by-four against the side of his head.

***

"Do you have to be so rough?" Koni Handler whined, trying to pull away from the arm that Reny had wrapped around her waist to keep her upright. "My side hurts.

Reny resisted the urge to remove her arm and allow Koni to drop to the crumbling cement that had once been a parking lot.

"You want to get caught?" she muttered, continuing to half-drag the woman toward the pile of pylons as she texted her commander for backup.

All she wanted was to get the woman into the safety of her car so she could return to the warehouse.

Her last glimpse of Sebastian had been him confronting the two men with an arrogant confidence, but she was anxious to return to make sure he didn't do something stupid.

She didn't know much about the stubborn Pantera, but she suspected that he could very well underestimate the danger of humans when they were scared. The sooner she could get back to help him, the better.

"God, no. Why would they be so horrible?" Koni muttered, her tone petulant. "I did everything they asked."

"Like lying to the police about who attacked you?"

"Are you a cop?"

Reny sent her an impatient glare. "I'm the person saving your ass."

The woman hesitated, as if considering the

possibility of pretending innocence, before she gave a reluctant nod.

"Yes, I lied."

"Why?"

"One of my regulars at the bar where I work asked if I wanted to make some extra money," she explained.

Reny's gaze scanned the shadows for enemies, her weapon held in her hand. Her senses might tell her that they were alone in the darkness, but she'd devoted the past eight years to ignoring her instincts, preferring to depend on her training.

"What did you have to do?" she asked.

"Let them mark me up like I'd been attacked by an animal and then go to the police."

Reny grimaced. "And you agreed?"

"They gave me five thousand dollars," Koni said. "Of course I agreed."

"How did you end up in the warehouse?"

"I—"

"The truth," Reny interrupted as her companion hesitated. "Trust me, I'll know if you lie."

"When I first agreed, I didn't know they were going to leave scars," Koni complained, holding out her arm that was marred by what looked like four long claw marks. The wounds were certainly deep enough to leave lasting proof of her stupidity. "I can't make tips looking like a freak-show."

"You tried to blackmail them for more money?"

Her lower lip stuck out in a pout that had obviously been practiced in front of a mirror. "They owed me."

"Yeah, and scumbags you meet in bars always pay their debts."

"Okay, at first they said no," she admitted, stumbling over a chunk of concrete. "Then last night they called and said they changed their minds. I didn't know they were going to try to kill me."

The woman burst into tears, but Reny ignored them.

It wasn't just her lack of empathy for a woman who'd been ready to lie to the police and start an interspecies war just for money. But she'd caught a renewed whiff of that strange sour smell that had been in the warehouse, warning her that they were no longer alone.

Dragging her companion around the pylons, she opened the back door and shoved her inside.

"Stay here," she ordered.

"No." With unexpected speed, Koni reached up to grasp her arm. "Don't leave me."

Reny cursed, unable to struggle. Not when she was holding a loaded gun. "An ambulance is on its way."

The woman gave a loud wail that made Reny wish she carried duct tape. "Please, they're going to kill me."

"Not if I kill you first. Let go," Reny muttered, grabbing the woman's fingers and peeling them away.

Then, slamming shut the door, she carefully eased her way around the pylons, not surprised to find the older woman standing just a few feet away.

"I'm FBI. Don't move." Reny pointed her gun at the woman's head. "Who are you?"

"Lady Cerise," she said, her tense expression visible despite the darkness. "You're too late."

Reny frowned. "What do you mean?"

"They've taken the Pantera away."

Sebastian? Fear thundered through her even as she desperately tried to hold on to her training.

She couldn't afford to be rattled.

"Why would I believe you?"

Lady Cerise arched a brow. "You're a Pantera as well, aren't you? Can't you sense he's gone?"

Reny stiffened. She didn't want to think about the whole Pantera thing, but the woman was right.

The faint awareness of Sebastian's presence that unconsciously hummed through her entire body was absent.

Shit. Her fingers tightened on the gun. "Where did they take him?"

"I can show you."

"Yeah, right," Reny scoffed.

The woman held up her hand, the bracelets rattling around her wrist. "I swear."

Reny narrowed her gaze, studying the thin face lined with age. "Why would you help me?"

"Because I am beginning to realize that I've made a terrible mistake. I thought—" She broke off her words with a shake of her head.

"What?" Reny prompted.

"It doesn't matter." The woman squared her shoulders. "Shakpi must be stopped."

Shakpi. The goddess they were discussing in the warehouse?

"What does she have to do with Sebastian?"

"That's where they'll take him," Lady Cerise muttered. "And I know where to find her."

"Tell me."

"No. You'll need me to get you past the guards."

Reny studied the woman's stubborn expression, easily sensing the woman was telling the truth.

"Fine. As soon as the backup arrives—"

"No, the minute they sense the authorities are near they will kill your man and scatter," Lady Cerise insisted. "We will have to slip in unnoticed."

Reny grimaced, but she didn't hesitate. She didn't have a damned clue how to fight a goddess. The FBI academy didn't have classes on defeating crazed deities that walked the earth, but there was nothing that was going to keep her from getting to Sebastian.

Why she was willing to risk everything for a man she'd met only hours ago was a question she didn't intend to waste time pondering.

"Let's go."

CHAPTER 7

Sebastian hadn't actually expected to wake up. Pantera who were stupid enough to let themselves be outmaneuvered by mere humans usually ended up dead. And besides, he'd never received the same tactical training as the Hunters. He was supposed to flay his opponents with his tongue, not his fists.

Which meant that when he finally forced his eyes open, he was actually relieved to discover he was lying on the floor of a small room that had been stripped of furniture, with the windows boarded over.

And he didn't even mind the aching muscles and tender bruises that revealed he'd been violently beaten while he was unconscious.

In fact, he was counting his blessings until the door was shoved open and a male with a lean face and glossy dark hair worn in a braid stepped into the room.

Chayton, the former Shaman, looked familiar in his traditional leather pants and a beaded vest. But it only took a glance into the eyes that glowed with a sickening power to prove that it wasn't Chayton who was in command of this body.

"Shakpi," he rasped in horror.

"Good. I thought you would never wake." A

humorless smile twisted Chayton's lips. "What's your name?"

Sebastian forced himself to a seated position, relieved to discover the toxin that had shut off his connection to his cat was beginning to wear off. He wasn't at full strength, but he at least wasn't completely helpless.

"Fuck you," he muttered.

Chayton squatted down in front of him, drowning him in a sour stench that made Sebastian gag.

"That could be arranged, if you want."

Sebastian shuddered, barely able to concentrate as the malevolent power pulsed through the room.

"Where am I?" he managed to rasp.

"At my temporary lair." The Shaman cast a dismissive glance around the room. "It's pathetic, but thankfully the Wildlands will soon be destroyed and I can create a setting worthy of a goddess."

Sebastian shook his head, hiding his stab of fear. "Never."

"Oh, it's going to happen," Chayton drawled, reaching out to run his finger down Sebastian's cheek. "Soon."

Sebastian jerked away from the cold finger, feeling as if he'd been tainted. "You don't have the power to defeat us."

Chayton chuckled. "I don't need to."

"What does that mean?"

"The humans might not have the strength or intelligence I would desire for my disciples, but they do have the numbers."

Sebastian made a sound of disgust. They'd

suspected that the cowardly attacks were being caused by the human disciples, while Shakpi plotted a more direct battle. Now it was obvious that Shakpi was personally responsible.

Obviously the goddess preferred to hide in the shadows and allow her followers to take the risks.

"You're behind the supposed Pantera attacks," he muttered.

"It's so divinely simple." Chayton shrugged. "A few dead bodies littered around the world and they're foaming at the mouth to destroy something. The Pantera will be obliterated in a month."

The cat inside him stirred, gaining strength with every passing second.

Not that he was stupid enough to think he could challenge a goddess.

For now, it was more important he gain any information possible and try to pass it on to Raphael.

"Why am I here?"

Chayton slowly straightened, folding his arms over his chest as he studied Sebastian with that unnervingly evil gaze.

"When my disciples called to say that they had an unconscious Pantera I told them I wanted to speak with you."

"Why?"

"I intend to savor the death of my sister's creations, but I will need a few loyal servants." Chayton's face remained impassive, but Sebastian could sense the goddess's smug arrogance.

"I'm offering you the opportunity to serve me."

Serve the goddess responsible for the death of

Pantera? With an effort, Sebastian pushed himself to his feet, the air heating with the force of his fury.

"You can take your offer and—"

"Careful," the Shaman snapped. "You get one chance before I allow my disciples to play with you." Chayton glanced toward the door, watching as Derek and Van stepped into the room. "They can be a little...rough."

Sebastian curled his lips in a disdainful smile. "I'll walk through the fires of hell before I'd bow to you."

"Fine." The power surged through the room, but even as Sebastian prepared for a killing blow, Chayton was heading out the door. "Have fun, boys."

Momentarily baffled, it took Sebastian a few seconds to understand Shakpi's abrupt retreat. She might be a goddess, but she was in a mortal body.

She was afraid of a physical confrontation.

That's why she was hiding behind her disciples.

The realization had barely formed when Van pulled his hand from behind his back to reveal a baseball bat.

"Ready to play, kitty cat?" the thug demanded, strolling forward.

Sebastian shrugged, well aware the idiots didn't realize his body was swiftly ridding itself of the toxin.

"Do I have a choice?" He made his voice sound as if it was an effort to even speak.

The goons smiled as they rushed forward.

With a fluid speed that no human could hope to match, Sebastian had the baseball bat yanked from Van's hands and whirling to his left in time to bust

Derek's skull open with one negligent swing. The traitor fell to the floor, his blood pooling on the wooden planks.

Van squeaked in terror, turning to flee.

He managed two steps before Sebastian grabbed him by the neck, dangling him off the ground as he whispered in his ear.

"Where are you going?" he snarled. "We've just started to have fun."

***

Reny kept her head lowered as Lady Cerise led them past the two armed men who stood at high, wrought iron gates and up the seemingly endless driveway. The older woman hadn't been lying when she said that Reny would never have gotten through the tight security without her.

Still, Reny kept her hand on the trigger of her pistol hidden in the pocket of her jacket as they climbed up the stairs to the columned terrace where even more men were standing guard. She was well aware that she was quite likely walking into a trap.

The only thing that kept her moving forward was the unmistakable awareness that sparked to life deep inside her.

Sebastian was near.

And he was alive.

The knowledge compelled her to remain just steps behind Lady Cerise as they entered the mansion and moved through the foyer into a formal drawing room. And gave her the courage not to flee in panic when she was hit by a pungent, sour stench that assaulted her senses.

With a muttered curse, she stepped around the edge of a large bookcase, hoping to avoid the notice of the slender man with a long, black braid and distinctly Native American features who stepped into the room.

She didn't have to be told that this wasn't just a man.

That there was some massive…spirit…contained within the body that she very much feared was the goddess, Shakpi.

She grimaced as a fierce power beat against her, barely resisting the urge to pull out her gun and start firing.

Thankfully the unnerving creature's attention was locked on Reny's companion, the narrow face clenched with disapproval.

"Cerise." The name was said as a curse. "Did I invite you?"

Astonishingly, the older woman managed a dignified bow. Reny was fairly certain she would have peed her pants.

"I wanted to make sure the Pantera arrived."

"He did." A cruel smile touched the man's lips. "My pets are playing with him."

Reny bit her lip, fear piercing her heart. She didn't know what they were doing to Sebastian, but she knew it couldn't be good.

She had to get to him.

"He's alive?" Lady Cerise asked.

"For now." The dark eyes that burned with a strange light narrowed. "What do you care? Your attention should be on causing panic among the humans."

"We have dumped the first body near the police station. It's already stirring outrage in the media."

"It's not fast enough. I…" Reny watched in confusion as the male abruptly dropped to his knees, his hands clutched to his chest. "No."

Lady Cerise stepped back, her eyes wide with alarm. Obviously this wasn't a usual occurrence.

"What's happening?" the voodoo priestess demanded.

Chayton grabbed his head, ignoring Lady Cerise as he tumbled onto his back, the odd power seeming to ebb and flow as he gave a cry of sheer frustration.

"This isn't possible. I escaped," he wailed. Then his back arched and he gave another earsplitting cry. "No."

***

Sebastian was stepping over Van's motionless body when he caught an unmistakable scent.

Reny.

Oh god, had she been captured?

Still holding the baseball bat, Sebastian raced through the maze of rooms, avoiding the guards who were focused on protecting the house from an outside attack.

Entering the formal drawing room, he easily spotted her standing next to Lady Cerise.

The tightness in his chest eased as his frantic gaze confirmed that she was uninjured. Dropping the bat he rushed forward, wrapping her in his arms as he sucked in a deep breath of her spicy scent.

"Sebastian," she sighed, pressing her lips to his throat before she pulled back to study his face with a frown. "You're hurt."

"It's nothing." He dismissed her concern.

She reached up to touch the swelling beneath his eyes. "Nothing?"

"Trust me, I'll heal." He studied her pale face. "How did you get here?"

"Not now." She pulled out of his arms, pointing toward the body in the center of the room. "We have bigger things to worry about."

Sebastian made a choked sound of shock as he realized that it was Chayton who was lying on the carpet.

"What the hell is going on?" he rasped, sending a suspicious glance toward Lady Cerise. "Did you do this?"

The voodoo priestess shook her head. "I don't have the power to hurt a goddess."

Sebastian ignored Reny's muttered curse as he stepped forward, leaning over the male body that continued to twitch.

"Then what did?"

Chayton's eyes snapped open, his hand reaching toward Sebastian. "Baby."

"Did he say baby?" Reny muttered.

Sebastian barely heard her as a red-hot fury blasted through him. He knew beyond a shadow of a doubt that the bastard was talking about Ashe's baby.

He fell to his knees, wrapping his hands around the man's neck. "God damn you, Shakpi."

The dark eyes were oddly pleading as they met Sebastian's lethal glare. "Chayton," he rasped. "I'm Chayton."

"This is a trick," Lady Cerise warned, but Sebastian suddenly realized that the savage power that had pounded against him earlier was now nothing more than a dull throb.

And even the sour stench had faded.

His hands eased their grip on the man's throat. "What's happening?"

Chayton grimaced, as if he were fighting some inner battle. "Shakpi is being weakened by Ashe's baby."

Sebastian sucked in a shocked breath. "She gave birth?"

"Not yet, but it's near." The man's voice was thick with pain. "The baby's magic is spreading."

A fragile hope began to bloom in the center of Sebastian's heart. From the second they'd discovered that Ashe was pregnant, they'd prayed that it would mean the return of fertility among the Pantera.

Now it appeared their entire future might depend on the child.

"Can it destroy Shakpi?"

Chayton gave a slow nod. "Yes."

"Thank the goddess," Sebastian breathed.

The Shaman reached up to grab Sebastian's arm, his expression rigid with fear. "No, listen."

"What?"

"Assassins," he hissed.

Sebastian frowned, wondering if he'd heard right. "Assassins?"

"They're coming."

"For who?"

"The baby."

Sebastian leaned forward, his hope being replaced by a crushing fear. "Where are they? How do I recognize them?"

Chayton's hand dropped as his eyes slid shut. With a growl, Sebastian grabbed the man's shoulders and gave his limp body a shake and then another.

At the same time there was a series of loud pops as the guards came rushing into the room, firing their weapons.

Lady Cerise swiftly turned to flee, while Reny calmly pulled her weapon and began picking off the henchmen one by one.

"Shit." Rising to his feet, Sebastian moved to shelter Reny with his larger body, steering her toward the French doors as she continued to thin out the herd of charging bad guys. "We have to get out of here."

"What about Shakpi?" she demanded.

Pushing her out of the house, Sebastian pulled his phone from his pocket and hit speed dial. "I'll have Lian gather the local hunters to secure the house," he growled. "They'll have the place surrounded and the guards disabled before the bastards know what hit them."

Reny hissed as a bullet flew past her ear. "What about us?"

"We're going to the Wildlands."

CHAPTER 8

Reaching the edge of Shakpi's lair, Reny and Sebastian waited long enough to ensure the property was encircled by Pantera and that neither Shakpi or Lady Cerese had escaped before they were running through the streets of New Orleans.

Sebastian set a punishing pace, forcing Reny to release her natural speed that she'd kept hidden for years. Then, confident she could keep up, he accelerated his stride as they hit the edge of the city and headed toward the bayous.

Not that she was going to complain.

She didn't fully understand what was going on, but she knew if there was a baby in danger she would run until she dropped in exhaustion to try and save the child.

Concentrating on putting one foot in front of the other, Reny barely noticed the thickening vegetation until she felt a strange tingling rush through her and she came to an abrupt halt.

Oh...god.

She shivered, joy rushing through her as she felt the soggy ground beneath her feet and the early morning sunlight that began to peep through the

Spanish moss draped over the surrounding trees.

Breathing deeply, she allowed the scent of rich, black earth and brackish water to fill her with…contentment.

There was no other word.

A delicious warmth pressed against her back as Sebastian wrapped his arms around her waist and pulled her against his chest. Leaning down, he spoke directly in her ear.

"What do you think of the Wildlands?"

"Home," she said, the word unfamiliar. She'd spent the past eight years in places where she never fit in, never felt as if she could ever reveal who she truly was.

"Home," he growled in approval, his arms tightening around her. "Tell me what you're thinking."

"It…smells right."

He chuckled, burying his nose into the curve of her neck. "Yes, it does."

She shivered, leaning against the welcomed strength of his body as she slowly, painfully lowered the shields that she'd kept in place for so long.

At first, she was overwhelmed. Christ. Her senses felt as if they were under assault as she truly experienced the world without a human filter.

Suddenly she could hear the thump of Sebastian's steady heart and the flap of a heron's wing overhead. She could catch a thousand scents that could be traced by single strands to the world around her.

The tang of a frog hidden beneath a rotting log. The sweetness from a floating lily. The intoxicating musk from the man behind her.

And then there was the acute sense of the animal that lived deep inside her.

An animal that was suddenly desperate to be free.

"Now that I'm here, I think I can shift," she abruptly said.

He skimmed his lips up the side of her neck. "When you're ready."

"I want to try."

Sebastian went rigid. "Now?"

She turned in his arms, meeting his worried gaze. "I know you're in a hurry—"

He cut off her words with a kiss. "We've already warned Raphael about the assassins," he murmured against her lips. "He'll already have the search going for the hidden enemy, as well as organizing a constant guard to keep Ashe and her baby safe. We have time."

"Okay." She stepped back, taking a deep breath as she concentrated on the sense of…well, the only way she could explain it was *awareness* that prowled just below the surface.

"Just relax and let it happen," he urged softly.

She did as he commanded, loosening her tense muscles and allowing her thoughts to float.

At first she felt nothing more than a gentle warmth that flowed through her, making her wonder if she was supposed to mutter magic words or do some sort of weird-ass dance. Then, without warning, an explosion of sensations blasted through her body, making her feel as if she was being ripped from the inside out.

Oh, god. It was…glorious.

Astonishing.

Shifting into cat form, Reny surged into motion, bounding over the boggy ground with a sense of freedom that made her soul soar.

There was a roar from behind her and suddenly there was a tawny puma with yellow eyes running at her side.

She didn't know how far they ran, she only knew that when she entered a meadow that was dappled with morning sunlight, it seemed perfectly natural to turn and leap onto Sebastian, tumbling him to the side.

His eyes shimmered with pleasure as they rolled across the soft ground, nipping and growling and even swiping his claws over her shoulder as they played with a glorious joy.

Reny might have stayed in her cat form for the rest of the day if she hadn't known that despite his seemingly carefree enjoyment, Sebastian was desperately worried about the lurking assassins.

They would have plenty of time in the future to indulge her long overdue exploration of what it was to be Pantera.

Closing her eyes, she once again relaxed her muscles, allowing the magic to race through her blood as she shifted back into human form.

A painful rapture that could easily become addictive.

Stretched out on the mossy ground, she was only partially aware that her clothing and even cellphone survived the transformation. Her focus was centered on the blazing awareness of Sebastian that was buried deep inside her.

It wasn't just sexual, although there was plenty of

lust burning with an incandescent heat in the pit of her stomach.

It was more the sensation of being connected to him on a primitive level.

Lying directly in front of her, Sebastian gently framed her face in his hands, his eyes dark with concern.

"What is it?" he demanded. "What's wrong?"

She gazed at his exquisitely beautiful face in wonder. "I feel as if we're connected."

A slow, unexpected color crept beneath Sebastian's bronzed skin. "Because we are," he said, reaching down to pull her jacket and blouse to the side, revealing four silvery slashes that marred the skin just above her collarbone.

She blinked in surprise. "What's that?"

"I marked you."

"Marked me?"

He grimaced. "My cat was a little…overenthusiastic."

Reny felt a small flare of amusement. Was he embarrassed? It seemed impossible that the suave, perfectly composed diplomat could actually be flustered.

"What does that mean?"

His fingers gently traced the silver slashes. "I've chosen you as my mate." His voice was low, reverent. "And I'm very much hoping you'll choose me as yours."

"Mates?"

"For eternity."

She should feel overwhelmed by the soft words.

Just a day ago she was a career woman who cherished her independence.

Now...

Now she felt nothing but a wild exhilaration that fizzed through her body like champagne bubbles.

Her fingers stroked through the tawny satin of his hair, recalling the beauty of his pelt when he'd been a puma.

"There's no doubt?" she demanded, her vulnerable heart not ready for any unpleasant surprises.

She needed to be absolutely certain that this gorgeous, insanely sexy cat wasn't going to disappear from her life.

A wry smile twisted his lips. "My cat knew from the moment I entered the office to see you standing there..." His fingers moved toward the buttons of her shirt, slowly tugging them open. "Your passionate nature buried beneath the starch."

Heat curled through the pit of her stomach, a hungry ache pulsing through her body.

"Is that why I wanted to rip off your clothes and lick my way from your very sexy lips to the tips of your toes when I first saw you?" she asked, her voice husky with need.

There suddenly seemed to be something incredibly erotic in the thought of making slow, delicious love surrounded by the bayou.

"The mating heat is only a signal that our cats are sexually compatible and that you're fertile," he explained, his finger tracking the lacy line of her bra. "The actual mating is a melding of our souls."

"Melding." She sighed in pleasure as his lips nuzzled a path of kisses just beneath her jaw. "Yes. That's exactly what it feels like."

"Reny." With a groan he found her lips, claiming them in a kiss that spoke of blatant ownership.

Which was just fine with Reny.

She belonged to Sebastian. Just as he belonged to her.

The thought had barely formed when instinct took over, and scarcely aware of what she was doing, Reny's claws emerged and she was swiping them across his chest.

"Jesus," he rasped in shock, yanking back to glance down at the four perfect rips in his shirt.

"Did I do it right?" she demanded in concern, catching sight of blood on his beautiful bronzed skin before the shallow wounds were healing before her very eyes.

Raw, primal satisfaction smoldered in his eyes as a slow smile curved his lips. "Oh, sugar, it couldn't be more right."

Reny watched in sizzling anticipation as he started to lower his head. The mating heat was flaring back to life with a vengeance. Then with a low curse he was pulling back, and with swift efficiency had her shirt buttoned and her jacket smoothed back into place.

"What's wrong?" she demanded as he rose to his feet and pulled her upright.

"Someone's coming." He kept hold of her hand as a male appeared between two cypress trees. "Hiss," he murmured.

The Pantera male, with dark hair pulled into a tail

at his nape and gray eyes, moved forward, his expression impatient.

"Finally," Hiss muttered.

Reny felt Sebastian tense. "What is it? Have the assassins been found?"

Hiss gave a shake of his head, something about the action oddly familiar to Reny.

"No," he said, "But Ashe has gone into labor."

Sebastian gave a short, strained laugh. "I suppose Raphael is a fucking basket case."

The other Pantera snorted. "Worse. He needs you…" With a shocking speed, Hiss was abruptly focusing his attention on Reny, his hand lifting toward her face. "What the hell?"

"Hey." Sebastian slapped the man's hand away, his voice filled with aggression. "That's my mate."

"Mate? I'm…"

"What?" Sebastian snapped.

Hiss gave a shake of his head. "Never mind. Are you coming or not?"

Sebastian wrapped his arm around Reny's waist, gazing at her with blatant devotion. "Ready for this, sugar?" he asked softly.

She leaned her head against his shoulder, giving a firm nod. "With you at my side, I'm ready for anything."

ARISTIDE

LAURA WRIGHT

ARISTIDE
LAURA WRIGHT

CHAPTER 1

Hot.
Smoking hot.
And by the smell of her, human.

Aristide tracked the waitress with his dark gaze even as he sent the solid green ball into the far right pocket of the one decent pool table at The Cougar's Den. Around him, a couple of his Pantera brothers hissed and cursed at the clean shot as they finished off their beers. But Aristide barely heard them. His eyes and his nose were trained on the wickedly hot human female working the room. The human female he shouldn't even be acknowledging, much less lusting over. Dressed in The Cougar's uniform of black miniskirt and white tank top, she took orders, stopped traffic and made tongues loll. Small, maybe five foot two, she had the body of a pin-up: round and lush up top and around back, where it counted. The perfect amount of succulent flesh for a horny male to fondle and kiss and grip and lick.

Aristide growled low in his throat and sank another ball with only a quick glance in the side pocket's direction. He was utterly captivated. As in, his eyes just refused to remain on anything but her for longer than a second. With her shoulder length, night-black hair and pale skin, she was truly stunning. But it was her large blue eyes that really drew him in. They seemed both highly intelligent, and unmistakably vigilant. An unlikely pairing for a Saturday night in The Cougar's Den.

Though a Nurturer, Aristide didn't work in the emotional or mental sciences, but he could always sense panic, confusion, anxiety and fear within others. Sometimes it was so close to a being's skin, it seeped out into the air around them. And this human woman, who he couldn't seem to turn away from, had all four infusing her delicious scent. He wondered why.

She started walking in his direction then, her gaze jumping from a table of older guys, to her cellphone, to some bikers, then to the small Pantera crowd around the pool table. If he wasn't mistaken, Aristide saw her jaw tremble slightly when she eyed the latter. When she eyed him. He purposely missed his next shot so that when she reached them, he could speak to her first. Human women were always a curiosity to Pantera males, but the Suits he was with tonight were notorious in their preference. Normally Aristide wouldn't give a shit. Normally, he'd back the hell off and let Roch and Damien make their not-so-subtle moves—moves human women seemed to enjoy and seek out whenever a Pantera male was in The Cougar's Den. But tonight wasn't a normal night, and for some reason Aristide couldn't understand or quell, this human female wasn't getting near his friends, much less landing on their to-be-fucked list. Hell, if Roch or Damien even tried to touch—

ARISTIDE
LAURA WRIGHT

Aristide's feral thoughts came to an abrupt halt as those fever-inducing hips he'd noticed a second ago swayed tantalizingly toward him as she rounded the table of bikers. Thank Opela by the time she reached him, his basic ability to communicate had returned.

"How are you tonight?" she asked in a smooth, feminine voice as her gaze flickered nervously from his eyes to his chin to his mouth.

"Thirsty," he said stupidly, his tone lower, harsher, hungrier than he'd intended. *What the hell is wrong with me?*

"Sounds about right," she said with a small smile and a bite to her lower lip.

Aristide's groin tightened with the action.

"What can I get you?" she asked.

He was about to tell her nothing, to go away and don't come back. And definitely don't ask his friends the same question or he might have an aneurism right on top of the goddamn pool table. But then her eyes slid upward, over his collarbone, chin, mouth. And those baby blues met his black stare, and he felt a pull on his guts and his heart and his dick unlike anything he had ever experienced before.

Attraction? Hell, yes. But this was unlike any swipe of attraction he'd ever felt. This was attraction times ten. No. Times a thousand. And without thought, the fingers on his right hand closed around the hem of his jacket as his gut, heart and dick instructed him to order the woman to drop her tray and slip inside his shelter of leather. Inside, against his chest, where it was warm. Where Aristide could keep her close and scent her. Where he could protect her—from the males in the bar, both human and Pantera.

But who's going to protect her from you, asshole, a voice inside of him whispered viciously. *From what you want to do to her this very second? This stranger. This HUMAN.*

"We have a few beers on tap," she began, her words a little breathless as she dropped her gaze and quickly checked her cellphone. "Or maybe you'd like something stronger?"

Something stronger…yes, and maybe hotter, too…something that involved her, naked, laid out on the top of the bar, him poised over her with a bottle of tequila in his hand and a lime wedge in his mouth.

Once again, Aristide made a growling sound deep in his throat, but he didn't turn away as he should. Didn't tell her to leave him be, as he should. He couldn't. Like it or not, comprehend it or not, this woman held him, and the puma residing inside of him, captive. His gaze traveled over her. Her exquisite face and her smooth, night-black hair…oh, and that mouth. He'd never seen her before, but she reminded him of someone. Who was it? Her dark hair, those shockingly blue eyes and that unpainted mouth that seemed as though it had been stained a deep, berry red.

His lips twitched as an image popped into his mind. Ah, yes…Snow White. A movie he'd seen as a child. She was Snow White in a tight black miniskirt and three-inch heels. Heels he would make her keep on after he stripped her bare and placed her gently on the bar.

A hum moved through his body, down below his waist where the evidence of his attraction was straining against the zipper of his jeans. Clearly, he'd been stuck in quarantine with Ashe's sister, Isi, for far too long. There was no other excuse for this impossible reaction. He'd been desperate for a female before, but nothing like this. And never for a human woman. He needed to get his shit together or get the fuck out of here before he did or said something unforgivably stupid.

"I'll take a beer," he said, forcing his gaze away and back to the pool table. "Any beer. But cold."

"Coming right up," she said.

Aristide knew that humans had a place in the lives of some of his Pantera brothers and sisters, but that would never be his reality. No matter how hot they were. Or how their skin or their voice or their scent called to him.

Teeth grinding against each other at the back of his mouth, Aristide grabbed the chalk from the edge of the table and worked the end of his cue. He was one of the males in his species who seriously wanted a mate, and—Opela be blessed—a family to go with it. And his mate *would* be a Pantera female. Looking, panting or drooling over a human woman was a waste of his goddamn time.

As he stretched over the table, he heard her taking drink orders from Roch and Damien. Doing her job. Her human job that had nothing to do with him. As his hand tightened around the stick, he tried to block the conversation out and focus on his shot. But it was impossible. His friends were being irritating pricks.

"I'll have a beer, beautiful," Damien said, his tone oozing sexual charm. "And your phone number."

"Smooth," Roch said, chuckling. "Forgive my friend here, darlin'. He's under the unfortunate impression that women find him attractive."

"And my friend here is under the impression that he's going to have a beating heart after tonight," Damien said on a playful growl.

Aristide lined his cue up with the ball. *Don't look over there. Because if one of those idiots is touching her…*

"Forget the phone number, gorgeous," Damien continued. "Let me take you out tonight. Somewhere real nice. What time do you get off work?"

"Sorry," she began tightly. "I'm busy."

"Busy for him, right?" Roch said with a smile in his voice. "But not for me."

"Not interested, but thanks," she said. "I'll get those drinks."

"Ah. You have a male," Damien said quickly.

"Something like that."

Crack.

The sound echoed throughout the bar, and Aristide instantly felt all eyes swing his way. *Ah, shit.* He was hoping everyone would think it was the satisfying sound of his last solid ball dropping into the right corner pocket. But he wasn't that lucky.

"What the fuck, Ari?" Roch said, all sexual heat gone from his voice. "You broke the cue."

Yes, the cue, and your attempt to hit on the woman.

My woman.

Fuck.

Aristide groaned at the asinine thoughts inside his

head. What was wrong with him? Why was he having such predatory, possessive feelings about a complete stranger? One who didn't have an ounce of shifter blood? And one who had basically said she was taken? He needed to get out of here. Forget the beer, forget the game.

His eyes came up, narrowed on the Suits. Both Roch and Damien were staring at him like he was crazy. The woman, however, was a few feet away, her gaze completely focused on the screen of her cellphone. She looked pale as shit, and that foursome of emotions was coming off of her in waves now. Panic, confusion, anxiety and fear—all drifting into Aristide's nostrils.

Aristide dug into his pocket for some cash. After weeks of being locked up with Ashe's sister, testing blood sample after blood sample, hypothesizing until his brain felt close to exploding, all he'd wanted to do was have a night off, a few drinks and a game of pool with some knuckleheads. Not cause a scene, driven by his overwhelming desire for a woman who shouldn't even be on his radar.

"I'm out of here," he mumbled, placing the broken cue down on the table and tossing a few more bills than necessary to cover the damage. "Sorry about that."

Aristide heard both males call after him as he headed for the door, but he didn't so much as slow his pace. Heat and desire and confusion and ire were barreling through him at top speed, and he needed some cold air on his skin. Then maybe he needed to get laid. Bury himself inside a willing and warm

Pantera female for a few hours and get his sanity back again. Shit, he had a few doors he could knock on. And an empty house he could use.

He busted out of the front door and into the cool autumn air. The moon was full overhead, lighting the landscape of half-full parking lot in a pale, yellow glow. Sex had always been easy, hot and fun. But it seemed like lately, ever since his sister had mated his best friend and moved out of their family house, Aristide had wanted something else to go along with that heat, that fun. Something lasting and real. Something that filled his empty house, and shit, his empty heart. A true Pantera mating. It was something he wasn't about to find in The Cougar's Den. He needed to return to the Wildlands where he belonged.

As he headed down the steps and into the parking lot, something caught his peripheral vision and he turned. A woman, he thought. No. It was *the* woman. His waitress. Snow White. He paused near a black pick-up truck and watched as she rounded the corner of the bar and walked swiftly toward a rusted green hatchback. Was she done with her work already? And where was she going in such a rush? Home? *To her male?* he ground out inside his mind. Damn, he despised how much his body screamed at him to go after her, question her, convince her to look for comfort and pleasure elsewhere. With him.

She was talking animatedly on her cellphone, while searching her purse for something. A moment later, she fished out a set of keys, her hand shaking terribly as she tried to slip one into the lock of her car door. Something rippled through Aristide as he remembered her face in the bar, the worry in her eyes, the fear in her scent, the constant checking of her cellphone. Was she in trouble?

His puma scratched at his insides, but Aristide shoved the cat away. He shouldn't be concerned about her. No matter what his mind said or his dick begged for, she wasn't for him. She belonged to someone else. A human male, no doubt.

Yet Aristide remained where he was, watching as she slipped inside her vehicle, hurriedly backed out of the space and hauled ass out of the parking lot. Yes, something was wrong.

Aristide's gaze flickered toward the bayou in the distance, the Wildlands where he should be headed, first on foot, then on paws. Then a sound yanked his attention back. Another car had pulled out directly after the woman, and was following her way too closely to be anything but a problem.

"Shit," he uttered as he abandoned all reason and sense and left the shelter of the truck.

He sprinted across the lot, his puma hovering close to the edge of his skin. Keeping up with a vehicle for any length of time wasn't going to be possible, but they were in town and things moved slower with stop signs and traffic lights. Eyes narrowed and vigilant in the moonlight, Aristide ran, faster than he'd ever run before. Over potholes and uneven pavement, the taillights of the car following her blinking scarlet, beckoning him forward. As they hit a red light and a few stopped cars, the woman veered into the empty turn lane. Tires squealed as both cars took the turn at too high a speed.

ARISTIDE
LAURA WRIGHT

His puma driving him, Aristide rounded the corner. He was nearly to the hotel when the sudden and fierce slam of metal against tree trunk erupted in the air. His heart dropped into his shoes, and without forethought he raced forward, uncaring, not stopping until he had the woman's car door open and her unconsciousness body in his arms.

"Come on," he whispered way too goddamn frantically for the total stranger in his grasp. "Wake up. Look at me. Please."

On his knees near the door, Aristide stared down at her. She had a gash on her forehead and she looked far too pale for his liking, but her breathing wasn't labored.

"Shit," he cursed when she remained still. "Come on, Female. Open your eyes and look at me."

Behind Aristide, car doors opened and slammed shut, and in an instant, it all rushed back to him. And to his puma, as well. Someone was after this woman.

A fierce and feral growl vibrated in his throat and he eased her closer to his chest as he prepared himself for a battle. It was illogical and strange, but he knew he'd fight to the death for this female. And that would take awhile. A Pantera male didn't die easily.

"Ari?" came a voice Aristide recognized instantly. "What the hell are you doing here?"

Ice froze the blood in Aristide's veins. Coming to a stop beside him, towering over him, was the leader of the Hunters. Parish. *What the hell?* And beside him was his sister, Keira, and another massive, dark-haired Hunter called Lian. They were all staring down at him nonplussed, the moon overhead illuminating their stern body language and expressions. All three were in pure Hunter mode.

Suspicious and massively protective of the woman in his arms, Aristide bared his teeth at them and hissed, "You answer first. What are you doing here?"

Parish knocked his chin in the direction of the woman in Aristide's arms. "We've come for her."

Aristide's wariness deepened. "Why? She's a human."

"Yes," Lian said with a fierce glare. "And our enemy."

Enemy? The word slid through Aristide's gut, hot and painful. Yet his arms only tightened around the woman. He had no idea what she'd done—or what the Pantera believed she'd done—but in that moment it didn't matter. He and his puma would protect her, no matter what.

"Release her, Aristide," Keira said in calm but authoritative voice. "Release her and walk away. Let us take care of this."

Aristide leapt to his feet. The sound that rumbled in his chest, then erupted from his throat and echoed down the deserted street, was so low and so terrible, both male Hunters stepped back.

"That's right," he snarled at them, his puma screaming to emerge. "Keep backing up, shifters. All the way to your vehicle. Then get inside, start the engine and return to the Wildlands. Because this woman will not be touched by anyone but me."

CHAPTER 2

The first thought Katherine Burke had when she awoke was: *Am I dead?* Followed closely by: *No, I can't be. I can't leave Noah.*

Panic struck her and she tried to move, to sit up, but strong, gentle hands held her down.

"Easy," came a voice she recognized. "You're all right."

Forcing her eyes open, she groaned at the intense light that instantly shrank her pupils and caused her head to ache. "Too bright. Please."

The hands left her, and in seconds she heard a click and felt the shocking burst of light recede. Blinking to gain back her vision, Kat took in her surroundings. It was still night, the intense light obviously coming from a bright lamp. She was in a hospital room. Everything was white and sterile, and as her heart kicked against her ribs, her mind bent back to remember what had gotten her here. It didn't take long for the chase and the accident to come back. Oh, god. Someone was after her. One of those cat shifters she'd written about. No. That she'd lied about.

"How are you feeling?"

On a gasp, her head came around and her eyes

made contact with the man from The Cougar's Den. One of the pool players. Mr. Cold Beer. He was in the same clothes, minus the leather jacket. Her gaze rolled over him. Tall, broad, shockingly handsome with short, thick sandy brown hair and black eyes. Her heart kicked. *Cat's eyes*. Yes, she remembered. He was one of them. The Pantera. Which meant what exactly? She glanced around again. On second look, the hospital room seemed different than the rooms she'd seen before. Her breath stalled in her lungs. Was she in the Wildlands?

"Do you remember what happened to you?" he asked, his voice so husky, so male, Kat felt its vibration all through her body.

Her heart beating furiously inside her chest now, Kat nodded.

Light brown eyebrows raised over deep, dark and curious eyes. "Do you remember me?"

The vibration in her body dropped low in her stomach. Good lord, how did one forget a face like that, a body like that? A voice like that? She eyed the white lab coat he was wearing. "Are you doctor?"

"Of sorts," he said. He glanced over his shoulder at the door, then returned his gaze to her. "Why were you running from the Pantera? Did someone threaten you?"

He seemed genuinely concerned, but Kat knew how men were. How they acted when they wanted something from you, and how they acted afterwards when they got it.

"This is all a mistake," she said, trying to sit up. "I don't know where you've put me or why, but I need to go home."

"And where is that?"

She hesitated for a moment, then spat out the truth, "New Orleans."

As the man came to sit on the bed near her waist, Kat drew back against the pillows. She felt breathless and warm, but not from her fear and anxiety. Up close, he was even better looking. He seemed to ooze strength and raw maleness, and she felt her curiosity flare. This was the real deal, and the Pantera males she'd written about—the fiction she'd invented—seemed positively puny in comparison.

"Listen," he began, his voice soft but threaded with warning. "Very soon we're going to have people in here asking you a lot of questions. Before they do, do you want to tell me anything? Who you are? Why you were running last night from—"

"The Pantera?" Kat said quickly and without thinking.

The man's eyes shuttered, and he growled softly. "You know about us?"

Pressed back against the pillows, Kat stared at him, her breathing shallow. This was bad. How could she be so stupid as to show her hand when she might've gotten out of here? This man—it was him—he unnerved her, made her drop her guard. Even back at The Cougar's Den she'd felt that from him.

"Shit…" The man sighed. "So what they said is true. You wrote a story about us for an online magazine?

She didn't answer. "You can't hold me here."

"Can't we? After all you said about us in that article? Calling us monsters who eat children?" He chuckled darkly. "Saying that we are not magical beings at all, but a cult of sociopaths?"

Panic flooded Kat's body, and she glanced around the room. There had to be a way out of here. A way to escape.

"What do you say to this, Katherine Burke?"

Her eyes darted back to him. One brow lifted, his gorgeous face tight with tension.

"Yes. I know your name." He leaned toward her. "How are you going to fix this? These lies you told? These families you've put in danger?"

Kat's eyes widened and her heart stalled. "Danger? What are you talking about?"

"Ah," came a female voice from the doorway. "The guards told us she was awake."

Both Kat and the male turned to see three people walk into the room. They were tall and fierce, even the one female, and dressed very causally in faded jeans and tank tops. The lean muscles on each made Kat's breath catch.

"What do you want from me?" Kat said slowly, fearfully.

The female spoke first. "Besides telling the entire world you lied about us? Immediately and on camera?"

Kat shook her head. "I can't do that."

"Why the hell not?" the woman growled, moving toward her.

But the man who sat on Kat's bed was already on his feet and standing in the woman's way. "Calm down, Keira."

"Fuck you, Aristide," she said. "We need answers."

"Why did you spread those lies, Miss Burke?" asked one of the men behind Keira. He had gold eyes, long black hair and scars near his right ear and mouth.

Keira shook her head. "It was just a satire piece. Like The Onion."

No matter how scared she was, or how much she hated herself for the article she was forced to write, she couldn't tell them the truth. Not if she wanted to see Noah again.

"And yet you won't tell the world that," Keira spat back.

Kat remained tight-lipped. She had to find a way out of here. But if she truly was in the Wildlands, how would escape even be possible? She had no idea where she was, or how far it was to the outside world.

"Who are you working for, Miss Burke?" the golden-eyed man asked, his calm demeanor unnerving her. "Because even though you have no tattoo, no Mark of Shakpi on your body, we know you must be working for our enemies. The ones who are desperate to tell the human world to be afraid of us, to attack us."

Oh, god. Was that true? Was that why Marco had forced her to do this? Was the man called Aristide right? Would she truly be hurting families? And what was the Mark of Shakpi?

"I work for the Jefferson Post," she said, shaking her head against the desire to tell the whole truth, and the fear of what would happen if she did. "I'm one of their staff writers, and I wrote a satire piece. That's all. That's it."

"Bullshit," Keira said, flipping her off.

"Hey," the man called Aristide growled beside her. "Rein in your sister, Parish. She's about to get her ass kicked out of here."

Parish sniffed. "Good luck with that, brother."

"Fuck you, Aristide," the woman returned, her own set of gold eyes flashing. "You can't do that."

"You're in my jurisdiction now, Keira."

Her eyes narrowed and she cocked her head, studying him. "You obviously have a hard-on for this human, but it isn't going to get in the way of our investigation."

Kat's eyes lifted to Aristide. He stood beside her bed, his expression hard, resolute, his body language screaming defensiveness. What was Keira talking about? A hard-on for her? Was this man interested in her? And why did that idea make her entire body hum?

"Okay, let's take a breath everyone," Parish said, though his face and expression were tight with tension as he turned his gaze on Kat. "Will you or will you not recant your story publically, Miss Burke?"

"I will not," she said softly. *I can't.*

"Then you will stay in the Wildlands until we have answers to our questions."

Ice raced into her veins and her breath caught in her throat. "You have your answers."

He shook his head. "We want the truth. Names. Locations. The plan."

"There is no plan!" Kat burst out, sitting up completely now, ignoring the slight pain in her head. "I don't know about any plan!"

"Okay," Aristide growled, placing his hand on her shoulder. "That's enough."

"You know something," Keira hissed, coming to the edge of the bed.

Aristide growled at her. "She needs to rest, Hunter."

Hunter? Confusion mingled with the fear, and the shame inside Kat.

"You said she was fine, Ari," Parish said tightly, his golden eyes narrowed.

"Nothing serious, nothing's broken. But she's had a shock. Give her some time."

"We don't have much of that, and you know it," Parish said darkly.

The room seemed to grow cold as everyone in it fell silent. Kat looked from face to face. Worry and hope etched each taut expression. What was happening? What had that bastard Marco gotten her into?

Checking his phone, the man behind Parish, who had been quiet up until that point, spoke in a harsh whisper. "We have a possible breach at the south border."

Parish cursed. "How many?"

"Seems to be a single." He shrugged. "Could be another lost traveler."

"Or it could be because of her." Keira glared at Kat, pushing away from the end of the bed.

"Out," Aristide growled.

"Fine," Keira muttered. "But we'll be back."

As all three of them filed out of the room, Kat released the breath she'd been holding since they walked in, and dropped back against the pillows. She was so lost. Deeply in trouble. How in the world was she going to get out of this unscathed?

She turned to Aristide, to the one person who had championed her, and offered a very sincere, "Thank you."

"Don't thank me," he answered, his eyes still pinned to the door. "Thank my puma. I believe he's the one who can't resist protecting you."

"Your puma?" she repeated, confused.

He didn't elaborate further. "Rest, female. You're going to need it." He headed for the door, adding, "And don't try to escape. There are guards at every exit."

Kat opened her mouth to respond, but no words came out. Only a puff of air. In the doorway, the man called Aristide had completely disappeared, and in his place stood the most beautiful and terrifying cat Katherine had ever seen. It was large and had sandy brown just like…

Oh, god. She'd known…she'd known this. Maybe not exactly believed it, but she'd known that the Pantera were shape shifters. But to see it…actually witness the transformation…have it confirmed.

She covered her mouth and watched as he stalked out the door, his massive head held high and proud, his thick tail twitching.

***

Hiss cased the perimeter of the small house on Geradon Street, wishing he was about five miles west, inside the borders of the Wildlands, and able to access his puma. He never felt as powerful without it. But this was where he needed to be, and this was how Parish, Raphael and the elders wanted it. Shakpi and her accomplice locked up nice and tight where her disciples couldn't find her. And even though the goddess was unconscious, the Pantera didn't trust that her devastating magic couldn't unfold at any second.

"You two stay here," Hiss commanded the two Pantera guards who were stationed at the back of the house. "Rage and Elise, you take the front. One at the door, one patrolling. And try to be inconspicuous."

"And inside the house?" Elise asked him.

Hiss raised one eyebrow at the pale blond Hunter. "I'll be guarding the prisoners myself."

The female nodded and took off with her partner. With Hiss, there was no questioning, no suspicion. He was trusted and respected by all.

So foolish. So goddamn foolish. To trust him or any Pantera. Because, truly, they were all capable of treachery.

Hiss entered the small, one bedroom home and headed for the door to the basement. The Pantera had made a practice of this, buying land, houses, all over the United States to use for their particular purposes. Hiding, escape, holding prisoners. This property was a brand new acquisition. To keep the Pantera's enemies close—but not too close.

Hiss descended the short flight of stairs, lit only by a single bulb hanging from the ceiling. The cold space was sparse, dank, and housed two side-by-side cages. Both of which were occupied.

Hiss's gaze moved over the human male, Chayton, who had been taken over by Shakpi several weeks ago. The male was still unconscious after his recent attempts to flush the goddess from his body, but Hiss knew that the powerful spirit still dwelled within him, hovering just beneath the surface of the male's aging skin, waiting for its chance. It would be Hiss's job to assist in her awakening. Just as soon as they had the blood of the child.

"Do your kind know you're a traitor yet?"

Hiss turned sharply at the interruption to his thoughts, his eyes narrowing on the woman in the other cell. "The only traitor here is you, Cerise." He clucked his tongue. "Leading that female to where Shakpi was holding her mate captive? You are as good as dead when she wakes."

The silver-haired woman with the sharp eyes shrugged. "Perhaps. But at least I won't die a fool. Like you."

Hiss laughed. He was no fool. Ruthless and without mercy, yes, But not a fool.

"I realized too late that Shakpi was only using me," Lady Cerise muttered, her fingers closing around the bars of her cage. "She was never going to grant me the power she dangled in front of me daily."

"See, that's the difference between us," Hiss stated evenly. "I'm not looking for power. Only justice."

Her stoic gaze connected with his. "And this is justice? Allowing a Pantera infant to be killed before it even takes its first breath?"

A painful heat snaked through Hiss's body. The death of Ashe's child would cause him no amount of grieving. He knew that. He knew he was about to become a monster. But it was justice. The deep and abiding pain the Pantera had caused him when they'd sacrificed his entire family to keep themselves hidden still bloomed within him. He was without anyone because of the Pantera. His Diplomat parents and his sister had been exposed to the human world, and instead of bringing them home, sheltering them, the Pantera leaders had allowed the three to be taken out, to be killed.

For the good of the Pantera.

He growled low and hateful in his throat. Just as they hadn't stopped his family's death, Hiss wouldn't stop the death of their young 'savior.'

"You look tired, Cerise," he said before turning back toward the staircase. "But remember to sleep with one eye open. Shakpi will awaken."

CHAPTER 3

"I hate this," Raphael uttered, pacing back and forth in front of the door to the room that housed his beloved mate.

Ashe was still in labor, Isi by her side. The sisters seemed totally connected, supporting and giving power and healing to each other, and Aristide had seen Raphael leave the room several times to give them space.

Aristide eyed the guards who were lined up on either side of the door. With the threat of harm to Ashe and her child, no one was taking any chances.

"She's doing very well," Aristide assured him.

"It's taking so long."

"It's her first cub, Raphael. And a Pantera. And we all know better than to rush a Pantera, don't we?"

The Suit's eyes lifted. They were tired, but Aristide's words had granted them a flicker of humor. "I'm just…"

"An anxious father," Aristide finished.

"Yes. And seeing her in pain…"

"But it's a beautiful pain. One that gives hope to us all."

"Nurturer," Raphael growled half-heartedly.

"Damn right. And better than having to wear one of those silk cat collars." He grinned. "Or as you Suits call it, a tie."

Raphael laughed for a moment, then his eyes narrowed a fraction. "Do I hear correctly that we have a human woman in custody? Somewhere in this very medical facility?"

Aristide's body tensed. "We do."

"And is she working for our enemies?"

"Parish and the Hunters believe so."

The Suit's eyes darkened. "What do you believe, Ari? It was you who found her, wasn't it? And your judgment has always been top notch."

Yes, it had. But that was before his puma had set its dark eyes on a secretive Snow White in heels. "She is definitely hiding something, but I don't think she wishes us ill. She seemed genuinely shocked when she realized the trouble she caused."

"Then why did she do it? I saw the article online." Raphael glanced at the guards, then looked back, his voice lowered. "And it's not one of those bullshit tabloids no one takes seriously. It's reputable. My spies have told me that the humans are taking it as a call to action."

"She claims it was satire," Aristide said.

Raphael sniffed his disbelief and his annoyance. "Well, whatever it was, it's already made the humans who live in our vicinity, the ones who've always wondered about us, start organizing. Search parties, investigations. We can't have humans raining down on us right now with our enemies closing in, our magic waning, and Ashe in labor."

Aristide's nostrils flared as he inhaled sharply. "I know, and I'll find out the truth."

"How?"

"I'm not sure yet."

Raphael took a deep breath and let it out. "Well if you don't, the Hunters will. Any way they can. And they'd better." His gaze flickered toward the door. "I won't have a traitor here, Ari."

Aristide's puma scratched beneath his skin. It didn't like this conversation. It didn't like what the Suit was insinuating. All it wanted was to get to the woman again and be close to her, protect her. Shit, maybe even rub up against her.

Fool cat.

"I'm going back to my Ashe now," Raphael said with a nervousness that completely contradicted his normally hard-ass demeanor. "Maybe she'll let me do something. I offered to let her hold my hand when she was having contractions, break the goddamn thing if she wanted to. But she needs her sister…"

"Everything's going to be fine, brother," Aristide said with a quick touch to the male's shoulder. "And soon you'll be holding your cub."

The look Raphael gave him before he disappeared inside the room made Aristide's chest tight. Nothing was going to harm this little family. This new Pantera life. This chance and hope for them all to have a future. Damn, maybe cubs of their own someday. He had to find out what the woman knew, what was coming for them and when.

He moved down the hall with long, purposeful strides. He had a meeting in the labs in ten minutes with two of his pathologist colleagues, but he was going to check on the woman first. Try and get her to talk to him, tell him why she would write such lies about people she didn't know, or a world she'd only guessed at while working at The Cougar's Den. But when he opened the door to her room, he didn't find her alone. The guards who were supposed to be outside her door and window were instead standing over her bed, trying to pin her down.

Aristide's puma burst to the surface of his skin, causing him to shift in and out of his cat state. Adrenaline rushed through him. He started to pant and his vision went crystal clear.

He launched himself at the bed, growled at the guards. "What the hell is going on here?" he demanded.

Never in his life had he experienced something like this. He was in pure attack mode, and it took everything inside of him to rein in his fitful cat.

One of guards glanced up, his eyes going wide at whatever he saw on Aristide's face. "She tried to escape."

"That's not true!" Katherine cried out, fighting the female who was trying to hold her down. "I just wanted to get up, walk around, go to the goddamn bathroom!"

The male shook his head at Aristide. "She can't be on the floor, sir, not today. We can't risk it. We need to strap her down."

"No." This time it was Aristide and not his puma who answered.

The female guard turned to look at him with a

shocked expression. "Sir?"

"I agree she can't be loose on the floor," Aristide said through gritted teeth, keeping his tone as even as possible. "But I won't have her strapped down like a mad creature."

Katherine stopped struggling, but her breathing remained erratic and her eyes were filled with tears.

"Then, how—" the male began.

"She's well enough to leave Medical," Aristide said quickly.

The female guard's eyes widened. "Parish will not allow her to leave the Wildlands, sir."

"And neither will I." Aristide's eyes locked onto Katherine Burke. "She's going home with me."

***

Her mouth agape, Kat moved underneath the rose-trellised archway and up the path toward the one-story house. A charming, freshly painted home with several mature trees bracketing it, and a sweet two-person swing on one side of the porch. It wasn't the only dwelling like it in the lush Wildlands. In fact, Kat had seen several of the darling cottages dotted here and there as she walked with Aristide.

"Not exactly the rat traps tossed together by savages who don't care about the sewage they live in or the hordes of unfed children running around," Aristide said, heading up the porch steps in front of her. "The near-animals who could break free from their land at any moment and go hunting in the human world."

Kat flinched at his words. No. At *her* words. God, she hated that article, hated that she'd had to say 'screw you' to her love of writing in exchange for such damaging fiction. But she couldn't help it. In fact, she'd do it again if it would keep her Noah safe.

As she moved up the steps to the porch, she took in the man who held the front door open. All six feet two inches of lean muscle and captivating presence. She knew now that his name was Aristide, knew that he was something in the medical community here, knew that he was an actual puma shifter—and god, she definitely knew that he was about the most gorgeous thing she'd ever seen in her life. But what she didn't know was why he'd brought her here—why he'd saved her from being restrained, from being an immobile prisoner in a hospital bed.

"Come inside, Katherine," he said in a calm voice.

Damn, she liked his voice. Liked it way too much. It made her feel safe somehow, no matter how insane that sounded in the situation she was in. Because no matter what, no matter where she was, she had to remember that she was still a prisoner. A prisoner who had to find a way to escape.

She walked past him into the house and saw that the interior of the place was just as comfortable and well appointed as the outside. Warm rugs and leather couches…desks and artwork, and a fireplace. Her heart sank a touch inside her chest. She'd always dreamed of having a place like this for herself and Noah. She wondered if, after all of this, after it was over, she could really have a normal life.

"Come. Let me show you your room," Aristide said, leading her down the short hallway that was lit by skylights. "Bathroom is there," he said, gesturing to the end of the corridor. "And this is where you'll stay."

This is the most perfect room in the world, she thought the very second she stepped into the large, warm and incredibly inviting space.

"My sister fixed it up as a guestroom before she moved out," Aristide explained behind her. "It's a little too white and has way more flowers than I'm comfortable with, but if I don't have to sleep in it then I suppose it doesn't matter."

"It's beautiful," she said in a whisper, taking in the rosebud wallpaper and blush-colored pillows.

"Good. Glad it suits." He was a quiet for a moment, then cleared his throat. "Well, I'll let you settle in, rest. You really should rest. Doctors orders."

"Wait," Kat blurted out, her back to him. "Why, Aristide?"

"What?"

She turned around and stared at him. At this man who, because of his size and muscles and intensely black stare, should be feared. But to Kat, his presence gave her peace and warmth, and—dare she think it—hope?

"Why are you doing this?" she asked. "Why did you bring me here? Why wouldn't you just leave me in the hospital, let them keep me hostage?"

His eyes remained a dark, calm sea. "Would you like to return, Katherine?"

She shivered. "No."

"Then it doesn't matter what my reasons are, does it?"

"Yes, it matters," she said with a touch of heat. God, she was so confused, so scared. She hated being scared. She needed Noah, needed to know he was all right and that Marco was keeping his word. Maybe she could find a phone, or borrow Aristide's cell. She'd lost hers in the wreck. But would he let her contact anyone?

"People don't do nice things for no reason," she said.

"I have no doubt of that," he agreed, leaning against the doorjamb. A sudden glimmer of amusement lit his eyes. "But I'm not *people*, Katherine. I'm Pantera."

His words—no, that one word—entered her body and melted like sweet chocolate. Oh, if only she could believe in the goodness of others again. That a man could be honorable, faithful…

"What does that mean, exactly?" she asked. "You must want something from me."

His eyes shuttered and he nodded. "I want the truth. And I want to protect you."

"But why? I'm nothing to you."

He started for the door. "Rest now. We'll speak about this later."

"You're not going to chain me down or lock me in?"

"There's nowhere you can escape to that my puma can't find," he called over his shoulder before closing the door to her room.

His words pulsing in her brain, Kat plopped down

on the bed, on the snowy white comforter. Oh, lord, she wanted to believe him. What he'd said about protecting her, and how he'd said it. He'd looked so sincere, like he truly meant it—like he might have some burgeoning feelings for her.

Idiot. Have you learned nothing from your relationship with Marco? Your mistakes? You cannot risk Noah's life, his future, by risking your heart again.

Katherine knew Marco wouldn't hurt Noah, not if there was another story possibility in the works. But she needed to get to him to tell him so.

Lying back on the bed, she gazed out the window at the lush green Wildlands, every leaf, every blade of grass glistening in the warm light of the sun. Night would be the best time for her escape. When Aristide was asleep. And when the beautiful Wildlands she'd trashed so successfully grew still and silent and cool.

CHAPTER 4

Aristide was a shit cook. Normally he grabbed midday meal with the Pantera outside near the bayou, but today was different. Ashe was in labor and everyone was on edge. No one wanted to sit still long enough to eat anything. And then there was the fact that he had a guest in his home.

A guest.

His nostrils flared. What was he doing, calling her that? Having her here under the guise of finding out information about the Pantera's enemies when, even now, his puma purred beneath his skin? The annoying animal was finally content for the first time since he'd scented Katherine Burke at The Cougar's Den. Aristide wished he knew what it meant, and how this would all turn out in the end.

Stepping back, he assessed the meal he'd prepared for them. Fried chicken, one of the Geeks had made for Xavier and Amalie. But, as usual, his best friend and his sister had brought some over for the poor, hungry bachelor. And there was fruit, and of course, bread pudding. It was the one thing Aristide could actually make with success, and without a kitchen fire. His mom had taught him how before she'd passed. Thought it was important for a male to know how to cook a desert. "Sweets to catch a sweetie someday," she would say. Just the thought of those special times made Aristide's guts twist painfully. He missed them. His parents. Even Amalie now. Shit, he missed having a family.

The scream that rent the air tore Aristide from his thoughts and made the blood in his veins turn cold. *The woman.* Was she hurt? Had someone gotten into his home?

Abandoning the food, he tore out of the kitchen and ran down the hall. When he reached her room, he wasted no time knocking. He wrenched the door open and burst inside. He found her fully clothes and writhing on the bed, moaning, twisted in the sheets. Midday sunlight washed over her face, illuminating the sheen of sweat as she continued to dream.

Relief snaked through Aristide's body. No one harmed her. He rushed the bed until he stood over her. She was still asleep, her mind conjuring fearful images or scenarios. His puma wanted out. It wanted to crawl on top of the mattress and lie beside her, lick her face until she awoke from whatever hell she was finding herself in.

Goddamn cat!

"Noah!" she screamed, lying flat on her back, her face and neck muscles tense. "Please, Noah. No! Don't take him!"

Aristide didn't know who this Noah was—if he was Katherine Burke's male—but he didn't care, and neither did his puma. He only wanted to soothe her.

He knelt on the bed, gently gripped her shoulders

and lifted her into a sitting position. "It's all right, Katherine," he said softly. "You're dreaming."

Instantly, her arms went around his neck, and she burst into tears. But her eyes remained closed. She was crying. In her sleep! Christ.

"Noah, I'm coming," she whimpered. "I swear I'm coming."

"Hush, now. Everything's all right." Aristide started rocking her like he remembered his own parents rocking him when he was a small, scared cub.

"I need him," Katherine cried into Aristide's chest. "I love him."

A quick flash of unmistakable jealously moved through Aristide as he felt her body relax, as he felt her come awake. And he was glad for it because having her in his arms, soothing her, scenting her, was doing something to him. And not just behind his zipper. He was connecting with her on a level that was inappropriate for the situation they found themselves in. She was not here for his pleasure, or to bond with him. She was a possible link to the Pantera's enemies, and he needed to release her, get up and walk away before he did something stupid. Before he pulled her even closer and forced her eyes to his. Before he told her that right now, raging inside of him, was an animal that wouldn't allow another male to get close to her ever again—touch her ever again.

"You're all right now, Katherine," he said almost formally, easing her back, placing her against the pillows.

"Aristide," she began, her voice still thick with tears. "I…I'm sorry. I was dreaming about—"

But Aristide was already on his feet and headed for the door. He didn't want to know. "It's nothing, Katherine. Nothing at all."

***

Fifteen minutes later, her face washed and her head clear, Kat ventured out into the hallway. She was mortified by what had happened, how she'd reacted, and she felt she needed to give this man—this man who had been so kind to her—some semblance of an explanation.

She found him in the kitchen, setting a small table with knives and forks and plates with delicious looking food piled on them. For two. Him and her, presumably. A sweet warmth coated Kat's insides at the strange, yet very sexy sight. This six-foot-two beast of man, with all his muscles and tightly caged ferocity, fixing lunch. She'd never seen anything like it. Experienced anything like it—like *him*. Total maleness on the outside and compassionate, nurturing soul on the inside.

"Can we talk?" she asked.

His dark eyes lifted to meet hers and he nodded. "Are you hungry?"

That question had so many different meanings to her in that moment, it was crazy, but all she said to him was, "Yes."

After placing a pan of something that looked absolutely delicious, and smelled even better, on the table, Aristide came around and eased back one of the wood dining chairs. "Please. Sit."

Really? Kat mused with a touch of sad humor. Manners, too? Seriously, this man had to have a rotten side. He had to be hiding something. He had to have an ulterior motive for the way he was treating her.

He does, Kat. He wants information about Marco.

Aristide sat down in the chair opposite her and picked up a chicken leg. "Dig in, Katherine. You need to regain your strength."

Yes, to escape, her mind tossed out quickly. But she pushed that truth back for the moment.

"You made this?" she asked, fork in hand.

"Only the bread pudding," he said, his eyes warm as he studied her. "The rest was donated to the cause."

"What cause is that?" she asked, curious.

His mouth twitched with amusement. "The lonely workaholic bachelor fund."

She laughed. "Ah, that. So, no woman?"

His eyes darkened. "Not officially."

The way he was looking at her, it was almost as if he knew what she looked like without her clothes on. Heat surged into her and pooled low in her belly. Eyes down, she stabbed a piece of the bread pudding with her fork and popped it into her mouth. The moment it hit her tongue, she sighed. It was delicious. It was *him*. This man. Warm and comforting, yet with every bite, more and more addictive. She mentally rolled her eyes—at herself and at such foolishly sensual thoughts.

"Do you have any family?" she asked him, abandoning the pudding for the chicken.

"A sister," he told her. "But she's mated. To my

best friend. She's the donator of the chicken."

"You miss her." It wasn't a question, and Kat wondered if she'd crossed a line with the observation.

But Aristide didn't seem put out at all. "Family's a tricky thing," he said, popping orange slices into his mouth. "You appreciate them more when they're not around," he added.

His words had Kat's shoulders falling, and her appetite receding. Something that didn't go unnoticed by Aristide. For the first time that day, his eyes grew cool.

"You miss your male?" he asked tightly.

She placed her chicken down and sighed. "Yes. I suppose he's my male. And I miss him very much."

Aristide also stopped eating. His jaw looked very tense now. "Where is he? This male of yours? Home waiting for you?"

Why was he getting so irritated? Kat chewed her lip. He had no idea what was going on with her little male. No idea how scared she was, how she counted the seconds until she could see him again.

"Is he one of our enemies, Katherine?"

The question brought Kat's head up. "What? Who?"

Aristide's eyes narrowed, the plate of food on the table before him now completely forgotten. "This Noah."

Enemy? Was he serious?

"Tell me, Katherine," he said forcefully, his glittering, black eyes narrowing. "Is he the one who wishes Ashe's child harm?"

"Oh my god!" She pushed away from the table

and stood up. "Hurt a child? No! God, no! Look, I had no idea why Marco wanted me to write the article. I had the connection to the online magazine and he used me for it. I hate that I did it." Tears pricked her eyes and her voice grew shaky. She couldn't stand him looking at her with that dark, probing stare. Couldn't stand how weak and foolish she was.

"Excuse me. I need some air." She turned from him and went to the door leading to the backyard. Yes, she needed air, but more than anything she needed his probing gaze off of her. He had a way about him that sucked her in, and made her feel like unleashing everything that was on her heart. And shit, she'd said too much. She prayed she hadn't risked Noah with her outburst. She blinked back tears. She was lost. So lost. She had to get out of here and see her baby.

Strong yet gentle hands cupped her shoulders and turned her around. And a voice, so soothing, so masculine, hummed in her ears.

"Look at me," Aristide said. "Please."

She didn't want to. She was afraid of what she'd see there. Pity? Attraction? Disappointment? Or worst of all, a mask of honor she'd want desperately to believe in. Her gaze lifted. But on that tan, sharply angled, devastatingly handsome face was only an expression of curiosity.

"Who is Noah, Katherine?" he asked, his warm breath moving over her face.

She couldn't stop the words, the truth. Not from him, and she didn't know why. "My son," she said, tears streaming down her cheeks. "My five-year-old son."

Aristide's mouth formed a thin line. "And this Marco?"

"Noah's biological father, and a mistake I made when I was young and stupid. I thought I was in love with him." She shrugged, feeling the weight of the secret she'd held onto lift. "I only knew him for a month."

"And the boy is with him now?" Aristide asked, his voice near to a growl.

"Yes."

"Does this Marco hold your child hostage, Katherine?"

The look on Aristide's face made Kat draw back. It was so fearsome, so unlike the man who had made her lunch just a few minutes ago. This was as close to a pissed off animal as he could look without shifting.

"Marco has no rights to him," she said. "He doesn't want him. Never has. And I thanked god for that every day."

"But..." Aristide ground out.

This was it. Telling him the truth—what would it cost her? And yet she couldn't lie to him. Something was there, between them now. He'd pulled her out of that wrecked car, and he'd held her close and soothed her during her nightmare. Maybe it was a foolish and inconvenient attraction, but neither one of them could deny it's amazing strength.

"Marco took him." Kat's voice trembled and tears rolled down her cheeks. "He said he wouldn't give him back to me unless I wrote the article."

"The article that makes us look like a threat," Aristide finished. Then his brows knit together. "The police? Have you gone to them?"

Kat laughed, but it was dull, sad sound. "He warned me against doing that."

A soft growl exited Aristide's throat. "But you've written it. Why do you still not have your boy?"

Kat's heart lurched and she shook her head. "He wants one more," she said. "It's why I've been working at The Cougar's Den." Her eyes implored him as the tears continued to fall. "I need you to believe me. I didn't know why I was writing that horrible article, just that if I didn't I'd never see my son again."

Aristide released a heavy breath and brought his hand around to cup her face. He gently brushed away her tears with the pad of his thumb. "I believe you, Katherine. I believe you."

CHAPTER 5

"She's no enemy," Aristide declared.

With twilight descending, he stood at the darkening shore of the bayou just outside Medical, the leader of the Hunters on his left, his sister, Amalie, on the other. As a Hunter herself, Mal was fully aware of what was going on both with the threat to the Pantera and with Aristide's houseguest.

"How can you say that after what she's done?" Parish asked him. "Everything she's written? Knowing none of it was true."

"Because I know her motivations," Aristide said. "Her belief that if she didn't write whatever this Marco wanted her to write, her child would be harmed."

"Maybe she just wants you to feel sorry for her," Amalie suggested. "Maybe she just wanted to get into the Wildlands, get another story."

"Well, then this one would actually be true, wouldn't it?" he countered.

Parish sneered, his gold eyes darkening to amber in the dying light of day. "I should never have allowed you to take her home."

The puma inside of Aristide snarled. "You could never have stopped it."

"Goddammit, Aristide, you're not taking this seriously!"

A deadly calm moved over Aristide. "You're very wrong about that. I will get you this Marco's location."

Parish's eyebrows lifted.

"How?" Amalie asked.

"I'm certain he's connected to the assassins," Aristide said, looking out over the moonlit bayou. His home, the one he would always protect. "Maybe we can stop him before their plan can be carried out."

"We?" Amalie repeated slowly.

He turned to face her. "I'm going with you."

Mal blanched. "Ari, you're no Hunter."

Aristide shook his head. "No negotiations. You take out the assassins before they can get to Ashe and the cub, and I'll get Katherine's boy."

"And do what with him?" Parish demanded. "Bring him here?"

Aristide nodded.

"We can't house a human, Ari," Amalie said. "Not for any length of time, anyway."

"Not unless she's mated to a Pantera," Parish put in.

"This I know," Aristide said in a clipped voice. "I'm going back to her now."

"Be careful," Amalie said as he turned to go.

"Always, sister," he returned.

But Parish wasn't done with him yet. "Why are you doing this for the woman?" he called after him.

Aristide stopped and turned around. Both his sister and Parish were backlit by the yellow moon. "It's for the Pantera."

"Why are you doing this for the woman?" Parish repeated.

Aristide sighed. Looked away. Then back at the pair. "I believe my cat wants her."

Amalie gave him a worried look. "Just your cat?"

"It must be," he said with a little too much passion.

"Why, brother?"

He cursed. "I am Pantera, Mal. You know me. You know what my plans for the future have always been. I must mate a Pantera. It's what I want." *No. It's what I used to want.*

A smile tugged at Parish's lips. "My mate's human, and she's helping another human give birth to a Pantera cub as we speak. Things aren't what they used to be here, Ari. Our past is not our future, it seems." His chest puffed up a little. "My Julia would give her life for me, and for any Pantera, I believe. She's my everything; my happiness, my soul. I'm so proud to call her my mate." He lifted one dark eyebrow. "With all that's gone down, there are many reasons to reject your attraction, your need for this woman, Katherine Burke. But being human shouldn't be one of them."

Aristide didn't answer. He couldn't. His past wants and desires were engrained in him. In the idea of a true Pantera mating. Like what his parents had. What his own sister had. Right now, he needed to get back and talk with the human woman. The woman who he cared for, certainly, and who he would help. But not a female he would ever call his mate.

He gave them both a quick nod before turning away, leaving the ever-darkening bank of the bayou.

ARISTIDE
LAURA WRIGHT

***

The moonlight clung to the tops of the trees, refusing to filter through and offer her safe passage. Kat followed the bayou, hoping, praying it led her out of the Wildlands and into La Pierre. Once there, she could find a way back to New Orleans. And to where she knew Marco was staying.

Hearing something, she stopped near the shore and glanced around. She'd never been in the bayou at night, but it was definitely not the still and silent place she'd believed it to be. Noises came from everywhere: the water and the land, and the sky. Kat hissed as a small nutria ran past her feet, the semiaquatic rodent heading straight for the bayou. Once it was safely underwater, Kat started moving again, waiting for that familiar sense of relief to wash over her, the relief that stated, 'You're fine. That was just a little animal who probably has very small teeth.' But what she felt instead as she jogged along the shoreline in a stolen pair of what she'd assumed were Aristide's sister's shoes, was a strange shock of guilt.

Aristide. He'd trusted her. Enough to leave the house without locking a door—or locking her up. What would he think when he returned? That she'd lied to him? About everything, about Noah? Her heart lurched. She hated the idea that Aristide would ever think she'd betrayed him. And yet, that was exactly what she was doing, wasn't it?

Betraying him to save her son.

The snap of a twig on the shoreline made her jump, and she picked up her pace. What was she going to say to Marco when she got there? Would he understand that being taken by the Pantera had not her fault? Was there any possibility that she could end this now? That her one awful writing mistake about the Pantera could be her last? That she could take Noah and just…disappear? She didn't even want to contemplate what might be coming her way. What her future, and Noah's, might look like if Marco was as 'above the law' as he'd claimed.

Up ahead, she saw an open area, almost a field, with high grass, and stopped for a moment to catch her breath. Was this the border? she wondered, looking around. Was she close to town?

But her questions went completely unanswered as a rush of heat hit the back of her neck, and a very male voice whispered near her ear.

"Big mistake, Katherine," Aristide said.

Panic flooded Kat's body. Large hands encircled her waist and he spun her to face him. Dressed in jeans and a thin black long-sleeve shirt that accentuated every hill and valley of muscle he possessed, Aristide stared down at her under the wash of moonlight. Lips pressed together in a frown, and eyes darker than the sky, he looked ominous. His nostrils were flared, and he was breathing heavily. She wondered if he'd just shifted, if it had been his puma who had found her, scented her, chased her down. Or the man himself had tracked her.

"I'm sorry," she said, struggling to free herself from his grasp. "But I have to get to Noah."

Aristide bared his teeth and his black eyes glittered like polished stones. "You think when you show up on that bastard's doorstep he's just going to hand the boy over to you?"

"I don't know, but I have to try."

"That he's going to be suddenly caring and honorable?" Aristide continued. "That he's going to be the boy's father now?"

Kat felt the blood drain from her face and she stopped struggling. "Don't call him that." She shook her head. "Never call him that. Marco was a sperm donor, nothing more. As far as I'm concerned, Noah has no father."

Aristide's face tightened. "Don't you understand? Going to that man could endanger Noah even more. What do you have to give him? A new story? Or the tale of your failure and capture?"

"Maybe he'd give me Noah if I tell that story, too," she cried out, hating herself with every word she uttered.

But Aristide didn't admonish her for her ugly threat. Instead, he loosened his grip on her and released a breath.

"You won't do that, Katherine," he said. "You don't want to do that."

"I will do anything for that boy. He and I…we're the only family we got." Her voice broke. "Don't you get that?"

"I do." His eyes moved over her face. "My life has always been about family. Cherishing the one I had and lost, and waiting for the one I hope to have in the future."

His words cut into Kat, so deep she sagged in his grasp. Why didn't a man like this exist outside the magical world of the Wildlands?

"Why are you doing this?" she asked him wearily as a breeze off the bayou ruffled her hair.

His brows drew together. "What do you mean?"

"Acting like you care."

"I'm not acting, woman," he growled.

"Then…why? What do you want from me?"

His answer came swiftly, and in the form of the most breath-stealing kiss Kat had ever experienced. One moment he was holding her arms, and the next, he'd taken her face in his hands and captured her lips with his own. Heat radiated off his body, yet his soft, full mouth felt cool. Kat groaned into his kiss and wrapped her arms around his neck, reveling in the feel of him so close. He tasted like fresh air and stars, and she never wanted him to stop.

His hands plunged into her hair, held the back of her skull while he nipped at her lower lip, than lapped at it with his tongue. Kat's legs felt like water, and her belly ached. Not with pain, but with a need, a desire, she hadn't felt in years. A desire she hadn't thought existed inside of her anymore. Something long dead, surely. Something she had refused to even contemplate trying to revive.

Something this man—Aristide, with his kindness and his fierceness–had resurrected with just one kiss.

Knowing it was probably her one and only shot, Kat gave herself over completely to the amazing feeling running up and down and in and out. She gave herself over to all the hot, wet sensations driving through her body. And when Aristide groaned and changed the angle of his head, deepened his kiss and let his hands travel down her back and over her hips to cup her backside, Kat pressed against his palms. She thought of the bread pudding. How every bite had made her want more. Kissing him, being touched by him, was like that—but times a thousand.

God, she wanted everything. She wanted to be on her back with this man naked above her. She wanted him looking at her, those amazing eyes of his, the ones that made her hope, gazing down at her as he pushed inside her willing and very wet body. She wanted him to say her name, over and over, as he came. And then she wanted him to hold her, whisper in her ear that everything would be okay before he kissed her asleep.

Aristide eased her forward, pressed her against his chest as he kissed her, hard and excited now, his tongue ruthlessly invading her mouth. Kat's breasts tingled and tightened, and her sex grew slick with arousal. She wanted him. She wanted him like she'd never wanted anyone. And when his fingers wrapped around the hem of her skirt and he lifted the fabric up to her waist, she nearly broke from his kiss and shouted, "Thank God!"

As cool air played over her ass, Kat gripped Aristide's scalp tightly and suckled his tongue into her mouth. Aristide responded with a growl and a quick, heady squeeze to her backside. *Oh, yes. Oh, god, yes.* The growl continued, moving down his throat, vibrating in his chest, causing Kat's breasts to ache terribly. It was only when one of his hands slipped inside the waistband of her panties and headed south, down over her buttocks to where she truly ached, that Kat believed she might know pleasure for the first time in years.

Panting against his mouth, she arched her back, giving him easier access to her sex, silently begging him to touch her. And when he did, when he found her drenched and ready, he slipped two fingers inside of her and cursed.

Electric heat flowed through Kat's body at the delicious invasion, radiating in all the right spots. Feeling full, feeling desperate, she clung to him, moaning and crying out and suckling his heavy lower lip as he slowly worked his fingers in and out of her. It had been ages since she'd been touched like this. And truly, her own hand didn't count–was a joke in comparison to this, to him. But she did know the burgeoning sensation of impending climax, and all of it was coming upon her now. Rocking her hips, rubbing herself against him, she wanted to scream at the rising tide of orgasm—tell it to go away, give her more time. Just a little bit more time. She even thought of begging Aristide to stop, but she knew if she was given a voice, she'd only beg him to continue—and god, continue hard and deep…and rough.

As if he could read her thoughts, Aristide quickened his pace, then drove up inside of her so deep, Kat gasped. *Yes. This was perfection. This was heaven.* Holding her close, Aristide worked that soft, G-spot close to her womb. That spot that would send her flying and crashing at any moment. But it was when he pulled his mouth from hers and commanded that she look at him, that Kat knew she was done for.

"Come for me, Katherine," he whispered on a growl. "Damn, if it's possible you're even more beautiful when you're aroused."

Kat stared up at him, her lips parted, panting. "How do you make me feel this way?"

"What way is that?"

"Sexy, and so safe."

"Because I want you, Katherine. I want you more than you can imagine." His eyes pinned to hers, the moonlight shimmering overhead, the bayou breeze rushing over their skin, Aristide thrust into her over and over as his thumb expertly massaged her clit. "And if you'll let me, I'll make sure you feel all of that and so much more."

Waves of heat crashed over Kat and her body stiffened. She didn't want it…didn't want it to end…

But she was powerless against the pleasure that radiated out from her sex. Her cries echoed throughout the Wildlands as she gave in, gave up, to the most intense and wondrous feeling in the world.

As her body bucked, and cream coated his fingers and her inner thighs, Aristide just held her steady, and continued to gaze upon her as if she was something amazing. As if she was precious to him.

Was she? She knew he wanted her. But was she precious to him?

The question undid her, exhausted her, and she dropped her head against his chest, sated. Breathing heavily, she whimpered, and Aristide kissed her hair and slid his fingers from her body. With gentle hands, he eased her skirt back down where it belonged, then gathered her into his arms. For several, wonderful minutes, Kat allowed him to hold her. But after awhile, as her skin cooled, the feeling of vulnerability and closeness was almost too much to bear, and she forced herself to move away from him.

With some distance between them, Kat found his gaze and held it, wishing this—whatever was going on between them—could last. No...could *grow*. But it wasn't possible. They were from two completely different worlds and life paths.

"What now?" she asked him.

He gave her a soft smile. "Come back with me."

Kat closed her eyes on a sigh. "Please tell me you didn't come after me because I'm your prisoner and you want information."

"I can't tell you that, Katherine," he said, his eyes studying her.

The pain that ripped through Kat at his words, his admission, nearly stole her breath. But she could still manage a terse, "Bastard." Tears tightened her throat and she backed up another foot. She knew it. God, she knew it. They were all the same. They all lied and used—

"But that's not the only reason I came after you," he said, his expression rigid. "Or, Opela help me, the most important reason."

"What?" Her anger still humming at the surface of her skin, she just stared at him. "What are you talking about?"

"I want to protect you, Katherine," he continued, moving toward her. "I want to find your cub. And I want to save the one who is about to be born here in the Wildlands."

Her mind raced over what he'd just said. Find her cub? What? Was he saying he wanted to help her? Help her get Noah? And if so, how could she believe him?

"Oh, Katherine," he whispered, reaching for her hand, lacing his fingers with hers. "My puma knew it before I did."

"Knew what?"

His eyes glowed black fire. "Please. Just trust me."

Her belly clenched. "I don't know you, Aristide."

He squeezed her hand. "And yet, you kind of do. Right? I know I feel that way. Shit, I felt it at The Cougar's Den the first time I saw you."

She shook her head, her fingers curling around his even as she warned herself to stop touching him. "But how is that even possible?"

He sighed. "Oh, the magic of the Wildlands is a curious thing. It exists inside every Pantera, and when a male or female recognizes their other half, the one they are connected to on a level that surpasses reason, that magic's released. It finds the match, the mate, and grabs on tight until both parties realize it."

He smiled at her. He was so gorgeous, so sexy, so convinced of what he was saying. But how could that be? He cared for her, wanted to protect her, help Noah…

"Keep that in mind for your next article, by the way," he added, then brought her hand to his lips and kissed the palm.

Kat shivered. Not with fear or pleasure. But with all that he'd just said to her.

"Let's work together," he said. "To bring Noah back to you, and to make sure that his sperm donor never gets near him again."

Kat didn't know if she believed in magic, or

god—if she even deserved it. But in that moment, her heart believed. In Aristide and all that he promised. She felt somewhere deep inside of her soul, somewhere she had always refused to access for fear of being hurt further, disappointed further, that he would do everything possible to help her and her cub. She smiled at that. Her *boy*.

Aristide broke away, releasing her hand. "Now, let's go home."

Home. No, she wouldn't think on that right now. Right now was all about getting Noah away from that monster.

"Climb on my back and hold on."

Kat's eyes widened at his words. "Your back?"

He flashed her another killer smile before dissolving completely into the spotlight of moon glow and reemerging as the gorgeous, growling, and fiercely protective puma she'd seen only once before. She wasn't used to his shift yet and her breath caught in her throat at his size and fierceness.

With a quick snarl, he made an impatient gesture for her to get on his back. Still trembling slightly from both the residual effects of her climax and from the anxiety of all she knew, feared, wanted and prayed for, Kat climbed onto Aristide's muscular, golden back and wrapped her arms around his neck.

The satisfied purr that broke from his cat's throat echoed throughout the forest as he took off into the trees.

CHAPTER 6

"Move and you're dead," Hiss uttered in his most deadly voice.

"Easy, friend," came the reply. "I come in peace."

Just outside the back door of Shakpi's and Lady Cerise's makeshift prison, Hiss had discovered someone camped up under the small deck. It had been pure luck that the Hunter had even spotted the male, as the bastard had been hiding incredibly well. All the way to the back under the stairs. And even more worrisome, he had masked his human scent.

Hiss pressed the butt of his gun a quarter inch farther into the man's soft temple. "How did you get past my guards?"

The male—the human—seemed completely unfazed by the weapon, or by the puma shifter who wielded it. "Shakpi chose well," he said, his starkly pale face splitting into an ugly smile. "You are ruthless."

Shakpi? Hiss's lip curled. "Show me."

The man's near-manic eyes widened. "Show you what, Kitty Cat?"

Hiss didn't even bristle at the man's attempt to ruffle his fur. "If you have true knowledge of Shakpi, then you know exactly what I'm asking for."

The man laughed softly, the movement causing his long, pale red hair to fall about his face. "Are you going to shoot me if I move?"

Hiss pulled the gun from the man's temple, but kept it aimed at his chest. "You can move. Just don't fuck with me. How 'bout that?"

"Sounds like a very solid plan," he said, reaching down and grabbing the hem of his shirt.

Hiss watched as the man yanked the black fabric up to his right nipple. Below it, inked into the ribcage, was the raven and the moon he sought. But something else caught Hiss's eye, something he didn't expect. Two slashes of red, of blood, across each raven's wing.

His eyes jacked up, and his gut went tight. "Who the fuck are you?"

The man's eyes glistened. "My name doesn't matter. All that matters is Shakpi. Has she awakened?"

Hiss hesitated, his mind rolling backwards. If there was one thing he remembered about his training long ago, it was the description of the very tattoo he'd just witnessed. Shakpi's disciples had warned him that if he was to come across a male with such a marking, he must do whatever was asked of him. Not to help Shakpi, per se, but because that male would be nearly as powerful as Shakpi herself.

"She remains unconscious," Hiss told the man, holstering his weapon and getting in fight position. He had a feeling if this male had wanted to, that gun at his hip—that gun he'd held to the man's temple—could've easily been turned back on him.

"That is no matter," the man said tersely. "We will take her there ourselves."

"Take her? Where?" Hiss had heard no part of this plan.

"Into the Wildlands." With his red hair and the strange moonlight filtering through the slats in the stairs, the man looked like a circus clown. A very powerful, very deadly, circus clown.

"Shakpi must be awakened," he continued. "And we will need the blood of that brat to both revive her and sustain her."

For the second time in two days, a wave of foreboding moved through Hiss. It was true that he hated the Pantera for what they had done to him and to his family. But in that moment everything inside of him—his puma—wanted to scream YOU WILL NEVER DESTROY US.

"Are you sure?" Hiss asked. "That the cub's blood has this power?"

"It is foreseen, traitor," he snarled. "Take me to Shakpi. Then go and get rid of your guards. Send them back to the Wildlands. My own disciples are here, waiting."

"If you cross the borders into the Wildlands, expect a fight," Hiss said tightly.

"But of course, puma shifter." He grinned evilly. "It's a fight we've been waiting a long time to engage in. One we expect—if my little writer monkey did her job correctly—to be followed by a human infiltration." His nostrils flared. "Now. Take me to her."

Hiss hesitated, a moment of second thoughts. But it was too late for him now. He'd crossed over his own traitorous borders long ago. It was time to see the job finished, and his vengeance taken.

He slipped out from under the stairs and motioned for the man to follow him. "This way."

***

"I can see the fear in your eyes, Katherine," Aristide said, watching her pace the wood floors of the kitchen. "And I swear to you, I will do whatever it takes to find the boy."

She stopped and gave him a pensive look. "I want to go with you."

"I know, but it wouldn't be safe or smart. If what you say is true about this human, Marco—and what I believe about his involvement with our enemies—he won't give a shit who he hurts as long as he gets what he wants. I need to focus on Noah. Without distractions."

"What if I promise not to be a distraction?"

Aristide laughed softly and went over to her. "You, beautiful Katherine, are destined to be my endless distraction." He reached for her, and this time she nearly flew into his arms. The action made Ari's heart muscle squeeze.

She nuzzled her face into his chest. "If this doesn't work—"

"Shhhh," he whispered smoothly. "Please don't do that."

"I'm scared. For him, and god…for you."

Aristide placed a finger under her chin and lifted her eyes to his. "Tell me you trust me."

She bit her lip. "I wish you could understand where I've come from. *What* I've come from. I haven't trusted anyone in five years."

"Oh, *ma chère*, that's no way to live."

Her eyes pricked with tears, but she nodded. "I still don't understand why you're doing this for me."

He dropped his head and kissed her. "Yes, you do," he whispered close to her perfect mouth. A mouth he had to claim. Just as he wished to claim her heart. He kissed her again. But this time with all the heat and desire and faith that was crashing through him.

When he eased back, he smiled. "If all goes well, I'll be back by dawn."

"Make it go well," she said on a stilted laugh.

"I like you in my house, Katherine Burke." Grinning, he pulled away. "Wait up for me?"

She nodded. "Be careful."

"Always," Aristide called back as he headed out the door and down the porch steps.

He was meeting Parish, Keira and several other Hunters at Medical to do a quick rundown of the plan they'd created. Outside the gate of his house, Aristide shifted into his puma. He was halfway down the road when he heard Katherine calling to him on the wind. He stopped and glanced over one massive shoulder, watching her run, his cat's eyes narrowed and his nose picking up her heady, yet anxious scent.

When she stopped before him, out of breath and face flushed, Aristide contemplated shifting back into his male form. But before that thought had time to truly take root inside his cat, Katherine broke out with the most perfect, most amazing, most needed verbal eruption in the world.

"I do understand," she said, her gaze pinned to his cat's. "I understand why you're doing this. I'm just so afraid to want it. To want you. Because I couldn't bear to lose you, or to have you turn me away." Her eyes grew liquid and supple. "I trust you, Ari."

For so long, Aristide had wanted a mate, a family. A true partner. And the last place he'd ever thought he'd find her would be the human world. But he remembered something his mother had told him once: *love knows no boundaries.* It would seem she was right.

His puma purred at Katherine, then rubbed its large head across her belly before turning away. With a howl of pleasure, of purpose, he broke into a run, knowing all the while that she was there, watching him until his tail disappeared from view.

CHAPTER 7

Kat had read, walked around the backyard and the front yard, eaten some leftover bread pudding, even showered in Aristide's amazing outdoor shower. Anything and everything she could think of to keep her mind from racing. But it was impossible. Her mind raced like a crazy person, and her pulse jumped every time she thought she heard something near the house. It had been three hours since Aristide had left, and she was losing herself in worries and fears about what was happening. Had the directions she'd given him worked out? Was Marco still there? Noah?

Pulling a blanket around her shoulders, she padded out to the porch and sat on the swing, looked out at the quiet, dark lane in front of the house. She should've gone. She should be there if something happened. She could go now, couldn't she?

Stop, Kat. God, stop right now.

She inhaled and exhaled a couple of times to get her bearings back, to push out the panic. Aristide was right. Having her there would be a distraction and possibly even a match to Marco's unstable flame.

Pushing off the swing, she was just about to head back inside, maybe try that book again, when she heard a sound behind her. She turned to see an enormous black puma kicking up dirt as it raced down the lane. Her heart jumped into her throat as it stopped in front of the gate and shifted into a tall, broad shouldered, caramel-skinned man with shockingly blue eyes and short black hair. His tense gaze traveled the pathway and eased slightly when he spotted Kat.

"Katherine?" he asked, raising one black eyebrow.

She nodded. "Who are you?"

"My name's Xavier." He opened the gate and walked in. "I'm Ari's best friend, and mate to his sister, Amalie."

Recognition dawned within her. Aristide had spoken many times of this man, and of his sister. "Is he all right? Have you heard from him? Anything about my son?"

He smiled gently, cautiously. "He hasn't returned, but Mal has sent me to stay with you."

Kat felt instantly cold, even inside the blanket. "Why?"

"We've been infiltrated by our enemies."

"Oh my god. Where are they?"

"They've breached the borders of the Wildlands and are moving toward town. Our Hunters will stop them before they get here."

"Humans?" she asked, feeling sick. She'd done this. She was responsible for this. She'd never forgive herself if the Pantera were harmed. Or the baby. She vowed she would do whatever it took to help them, to undo her lies.

"They're disciples of Shakpi," Xavier continued.

"The evil spirit who has one goal: to destroy the Wildlands." His jaw tightened. "Her followers are out for blood. They believe it's the only way to revive Shakpi and return her to power."

It was almost too much to take in, but there was one thing Kat understood. The blood they wanted wasn't from battling the Pantera. "The baby?"

Xavier nodded gravely, though his eyes shimmered with happiness and hope. "Ashe's cub has just been born. A beautiful little female."

***

A battle of distraction raged behind Hiss as he ran toward Medical, Chayton's body, near lifeless, in his arms. He tried not to think about what he was doing, what he was allowing to happen, and all the Pantera lives that were at stake back near the border. He just kept moving. The human male weighed practically nothing, making it an easy feat, but it wasn't the man's weight that was Hiss's biggest concern. If Shakpi couldn't be revived by the blood of Ashe's cub, she would certainly perish along with this man—the host who sheltered her. Hiss couldn't let that happen. If he survived this monumental act of treason, if he was going to out the Elders and the leaders of the Pantera for all they had done to his family, he needed the evil one's power to keep him alive and safe outside of the Wildlands.

All around him, dawn threatened to break, and Hiss quickened his pace. He'd created the camouflaged shelter he was headed for. Had scoped out the spot himself. It was perfect. Near enough to Medical so the blood could be delivered while it was still warm, but far enough to be hidden from sight.

His eyes vigilant, his nostrils widened for the scent of any Pantera who might be headed his way, headed into battle with the magic-laced humans, Hiss spotted the heavily wooded area up ahead. It was untouched, and he blew out a breath of relief.

Kneeling down, he placed the male inside the small shelter made up of leaves and bracken, wishing he'd brought something to cover him with. Chayton's breathing was worrisome. It seemed overly shallow and his skin looked ashen.

Hiss glanced up at the sky. The human male should've been there by now. What the hell was keeping him? Hiss would be discovered if he remained longer than a quarter hour. But the wave of concern that moved through him was overtaken by the sudden and strong scent of a Pantera he knew well. She was smart and cunning, and she was upon him in an instant.

"Hiss?"

Heart thundering in his chest, Hiss rose. He kept his body in front of the shelter. He didn't want to have to hurt her, his closest friend within the Hunter community, but the human male was on his way. And that bastard would show no mercy to anyone who stood in his way.

"What are you doing here?" she asked, coming toward him. "You're needed—" She stopped a few feet away, caught sight of the shelter and blanched. Her gaze slid to his, then back to the shelter.

Thinking fast, Hiss blurted out, "Shakpi awakened. I followed her here. I'm guarding her—"

"No," Mal said tightly.

Hiss could practically feel her mind working.

"Oh, Hiss," she whispered, dropping into a crouch.

"Don't do that, Mal. You have no idea…"

His words were ripped from him a rush as Amalie simultaneously shifted to her puma, and knocked him backwards. She was on top of his chest in an instant. Hiss had never seen her so feral. With a curse, he shifted too, and bit into her puma's neck with his fangs. Mal cried out, but drew back and battered his face with her paws, drawing blood. Rolling on the ground, fur flying everywhere, the two cats clawed and bit at each other, vying for dominance. Finally, Hiss got his legs underneath him enough to push her off. Twin snarls rent the air as both of them scrambled to their feet, then shifted back to their human forms.

Breathing heavily, Hiss growled at her. "I don't want to hurt you, Mal! Goddammit!"

A few feet away, Mal glared at him and spat on the ground. "You already have."

"Get out of here now," Hiss returned.

But she didn't move. "I trusted you with my life."

"We all trusted you."

Hiss whirled around at the male voice. Moving through the trees toward them were two Hunters: Lian and Rosalie. They looked ready to kill.

Panic swirled through Hiss. Could he run? Make it to the border? Fuck, no. Lian was one of the fastest males he knew.

"Don't even think about it," came another male voice behind him.

Again, Hiss whirled. This time it was Mercier who blocked his way.

The massive Hunter shook his head, his sable eyes flashing pure hatred. "You deserve death for this, Hiss."

"And you won't get that blood," Lian called.

Hiss turned back, utterly fucked now. Lian was standing beside the shelter that housed Shakpi.

"The cub is born," Lian said. "Healthy and beautiful. Your plan has gone to hell. And the one you're waiting for? He's dead." The male sniffed. "The asshole's name was Marco something. A real piece of shit. Like the bottom of your shoe."

Rosalie shook her head. "Nice company you've been keeping, Hiss."

Exhaustion barreled down on Hiss. Some of it from all the shifting, but most of it from the burden he'd been carrying for too damn long.

"The battle?" he ground out.

"Over," Rosalie said told him. "Two casualties."

Hiss's head came up, nausea snaking through him at the thought of a dead Pantera. "Who?

"Human. The disciples." She stared at him. "But you can bet your ass someone will find out about it—that human blood was spilled inside the Wildlands. They're going to be coming for us now. Maybe not today, but soon."

"None of ours were hurt?" Hiss said without thinking.

Mercier laughed bitterly. "There's no *ours* anymore, Traitor."

But Rosalie nodded. "A Pantera Hunter was hurt. An apprentice."

"Which one?"

"Why should it matter?" Lian uttered blackly. "You don't give a shit about us. You betrayed us."

"I was betrayed too, Lian!" Hiss spat. "So go fuck yourself!"

"What?" Rosalie asked. "What are you talking about?"

He knew it was pointless, knew they wouldn't care or believe him. But he told them anyway. "The leaders of our kind, Rosalie. They allowed my family to be killed all those years ago, for the good of the clan." He growled. "Where is my justice? I'm not the only traitor here."

All three Hunters were silent for a moment, then Mercier spoke. "Mal, you and Rosalie take Hiss into custody. Lian and I will follow with Shakpi."

"Oh, yeah, that's right," Hiss said, wanting to run as Rosalie came toward him, but knowing he wouldn't make it out alive. And goddammit, he had to stay alive. "Ask them! Any of you. Ask the elders. Shit, ask Raphael."

But they weren't listening now. They had a job to do. Hiss knew how their minds worked, because once upon a time he was a loyal Hunter, too.

CHAPTER 8

Kat was going crazy. Dawn had broken a good thirty minutes ago and there was no sign of Aristide. She and Xavier were both feeling the stress of not knowing what was going on. Inside the house one moment, pacing the gardens the next. No one had come by to tell them anything. No one seemed to be around. Kat was ready to beg Xavier to go and find out some news and come back. But she knew he wouldn't go. There was a sort of silent code between the males here, especially best friends like Xavier and Aristide. They looked out for each other, and Kat couldn't help but be moved by it.

"Coffee?"

Shivering in the gray morning light, she glanced over her shoulder to see Xavier walking down the porch steps, two cups in his hand. "No, thanks."

"Come on now," he said, holding one steaming mug out to her. "It gives you something to do. Something to sip and hold while you're slowly going mad."

He grinned at her on that last bit, and she laughed softly and took the cup. "Thank you, Xavier. For the coffee, and for the company."

"Anytime," he said. He came to stand beside her at the gate. "He'll succeed, Katherine. I know him like no one else. His word is everything to him."

Her heart squeezed inside her chest. Yes, she believed that. "How long have you two been best friends?"

"Seems like forever," Xavier said with a sniff. "Since we were cubs. I did think we might be headed for a breakup a short time ago when I fell in love with his sister."

Kat turned to look at him. "Really? I'd think he'd find that comforting. His best friend, who he trusts, and his sister."

"Well, it turns out he did end up feeling that way." His dark brows lifted over his extraordinary eyes. "But I was worried. That male is family to me, and I did not want to lose him. Nothing's more important than family." He smiled a very wicked smile. "You'll see."

Heat surged into her cheeks and she nearly choked out, "What?"

Xavier laughed, but the sound died away nearly as quickly as it came. He glanced past her, craned his neck and narrowed his eyes. "Katherine, come."

"What?" Kat followed him out the gate and onto the dirt road. For a second, she couldn't see anything. Dawn had broken, but there were some low hanging clouds about. But after a moment, she caught sight of something in the distance. Her heart lurched, then started slamming against her ribs. *No…it can't be.* Without another thought, she started toward it. Walking slowly at first. She thought she heard Xavier call to her, but she didn't look back. She swore she saw the cat she wished to see. But what of the boy?

She slowed, stared, not believing what she was seeing. Because truly, how could it be possible? Then she gave a muffled cry and took off. Running toward the puma, and its small, blond, five-year-old rider.

"Noah!" she cried, and barely gave Aristide's puma time to stop before snatching the boy up in her arms and squeezing him tight. "Oh, my baby. Oh, my boy. I missed you so much."

She pulled back and inspected him, every inch she could see, and when she found him perfect, unharmed, she squeezed him again.

Aristide was shifting, returning to his tall, strong, capable, honorable, wonderful self. And when he caught Kat's eye, he winked at her and gave her a grin.

"Someone's happy," he said.

"You have no idea," Kat cried, touching her boy's hair and his face. *Was he real? Was she truly this lucky?*

"Mommy can we stay here?" Noah asked near her ear. "For a little while at least? I don't like it out there. I'm scared. But here..." He giggled. "I've got my own puma protector." He lifted his head. "Right, Ari?"

"You know it, Cub," Aristide said with a playful growl, reaching over to tousle the boy's hair.

"We'll talk about that later, honey," Kat said, feeling slightly embarrassed. Aristide had been so kind, so amazing to her, the last thing in the world she wanted to do was put him on the spot. "Right now, I want you to come inside and get some sleep."

"But it's morning," Noah whined. "I'm not tired."

"Who's hungry?" Xavier called, loping up to meet them. He enveloped Aristide in a hug, and slapped his back a few times. "Damn. It's good to see you, brother."

"You, too," Aristide said.

"I'm hungry," Noah called out. "I'm pretty sure I could eat a whale."

"A whale?" Xavier repeated, his blue eyes going wide. "That's some serious fish food, little cub."

"Whales aren't fish, they're mammals."

Both Aristide and Xavier laughed, and the former ruffled Noah's hair again. Kat wished the moment could go on for hours, days… The jokes, the love, the family. How could she have ever written such things about such a wonderful place? She would fix it. Even if she had to deal with Marco. She owed everyone here, Aristide most of all, a good story. A true love letter to the Wildlands.

"Come on, ya'll," Xavier said, dropping an arm over Aristide's shoulders. "Let's go to my place and see if Mal's back. Find out what's happened and where we stand while we stuff our faces."

"Yippee!" Noah screamed, making everyone laugh again.

Aristide turned to Kat and gave her look so intense, so hot, it sent shivers of desire through her. But his voice remained as cool as the air around them. "No one's going to be able to sleep anytime soon. There's much to talk about, and much to celebrate." His eyes burned into her. "Right?"

She nodded. "Right." She wasn't sure what he meant. If he was just talking about their small party.

Or her. And him. Either way, she had to find out.

"Did I say how much I missed you?" Kat said in between kisses as she and Noah walked down the street next to the two grown Pantera males.

Noah giggled. "Yes. But I already knew."

"You did?"

"Ari told me."

Kat glanced over at the man, the male—the guy she was so desperately falling for. He was walking side by side with Xavier, but his eyes were pinned on her.

"When he came and found me in that mean man's house," Noah continued. "He told me how much you love me and that you missed me and that if I just trusted him, he'd bring me to you."

Tears pricked Kat's eyes. "I'm so glad we both trusted him, baby."

As she hugged her boy closer, she felt Aristide's hand at her back, guiding her, protecting her, treating her with such care as they all walked together through town.

***

A few hours later, Aristide led Kat into the house. His house. His family's house. A house that craved, and deserved, to have happiness again. For so long, it had been just him and Amalie. But now, Aristide was hoping for a fresh start with two humans he knew in his guts he didn't want to live without.

He closed the door and eased Katherine into his arms. She melted into him at once. Noah had been having so much fun at Mal and Xavier's place, he'd refused to leave. After eating more than a boy twice his size—maybe he had a touch of the Pantera in him?—Xavier had pulled him into a game he was creating on the computer. Noah had begged to stay for another hour. Which was a perfect amount of time for what Aristide had planned for his mother.

"Ashe's cub is well and safe," he said, gazing down at her, his puma purring inside his chest. The feel of her against him was making his body roar to life. "And your boy is well and safe, and will never have to fear that monster again." He raised a brow. "But what about you, Katherine? Do you feel safe? Here, with me?"

Her eyes sparkled with undeniable happiness as she gazed up at him. "I feel so much more than that, Ari."

A low, hungry growl escaped his throat. "Oh, I love when you call me that."

She grinned. "Then I'll always call you that."

Always. Yes, he liked that.

"Do you think the Pantera would allow Noah and I to stay for a little while?" she asked, a touch of her contentment, her happiness, stolen by a momentary thread of concern.

Aristide lifted one eyebrow. "Only mated humans can live in the Wildlands, darlin'."

It was as if her entire world came tumbling down in that moment, in that stupid comment, and Aristide felt like a giant asshole for chiding her. "Katherine, I'm sorry."

"No. No." She shook her head and tried to ease

herself away from him. "That's okay. I understand. We can go this afternoon."

Oh, shit. He was not doing this well. Holding her close, he allowed his puma a moment of possessiveness with a soft snarl. Then he held her gaze. "Listen to me, Katherine Burke. And listen well. Right now I ache for you so badly I can barely contain it. I need to touch you. I need to kiss you. Christ, I need to feel what it's like to be inside of you. So deep, we both lose our minds and our breath."

She stared up at him confused. "I don't understand."

"But first you need to know how I feel," he continued, his strong jaw tight and his eyes flashing black fire. "I want you. Here. With me. Forever. I want to mate you. I want to wake up every morning to your face, and have you fall asleep in my arms every night."

Her mouth dropped open and she stilled. "I want that, too. Oh, Ari, I want that more than anything. But are you sure? I'm not a Pantera female."

"You are my female," he said roughly, bending down and scooping her up in his arms. "And I'm taking you to our room and to our bed to make sure you understand that fact."

"Our room," she repeated. "Our bed?"

"Fuck, yes, Katherine Burke. Our everything."

He felt her shiver in his arms, knew that right then her nipples were getting hard. He licked his lips. "Noah can have the room you've been staying in," he decreed, moving swiftly down the hall. "Unless he hates the flowers. I'm not too into the flowers myself. So maybe we could fix it up together, him and me."

"Aristide?"

He stopped just inside the bedroom and turned to look at her. She was so beautiful. Her cheeks flushed with desire. Her eyes wide with desire, and a need for reassurance from him.

"You do want this?" he asked savagely. "Say you want this, that you want me. Because I want you and Noah more than anything. I know what you said about him not having a father, but it's not right. He needs that. And…I need him."

Tears welled in her eyes, and she nodded. "Yes, Ari. All of it. A million times, yes."

It was all he needed to hear. He stretched her out on the bed, then started undressing her. First her shoes, then her skirt and top, his eyes never leaving hers. But when she was completely naked before him, he drew back and allowed his gaze move over her, explore, covet. Oh, she took his breath away. Pale, long limbs, narrow waist, lightly muscled arms, full breasts with edible nipples that seemed to call to him.

"Mine," he growled, feeling his male self collide with his puma.

"Then take me, Ari," she said passionately, her arms outstretched. "I need you. I need you inside me. I've never wanted anything more."

Aristide wanted hours to explore every inch of her, kiss every peak and valley, lick every drop of sweet cream from her nearly shaved pussy. But when she spread her legs wide and showed him just how slick and pink she was, he couldn't be contained any longer. After all, they had tonight and tomorrow, and forever, to explore.

Aristide quickly stripped, then growled softly at her as her eyes dropped to his heavy shaft. "See something you like?"

She smiled wickedly. "Oh, Ari, so many things. But right now, I need you over me, inside me, against me."

He was on the bed in seconds, had her thighs spread a few inches wider and his cock sliding home before she said another word. Liquid heat enveloped him, and when she wrapped her legs around his waist and arched her back, he thrust into her so deep, she gasped. He dropped his head and captured her mouth, taking her gasps and her groans into his lungs. It was perfect, like fine wine.

"My Katherine," he whispered against her lips, moving inside of her, claiming her, taking her all the way to the brink of climax. "My life, my family, my love."

And when she cried out and exploded around him, Aristide went with her. Followed her over the edge and into a new and wonderful life for them both.

EPILOGUE

The small cabin on the isolated island in the Wildlands was surrounded by heavy flora, and a perilous swamp that had claimed a few unwary Pantera over the years. It was used to imprison those who had done the Pantera wrong, and those who couldn't control their cats any longer. Hiss belonged to the former group. The wrongdoers and the traitors.

Standing over the cot that only days ago had hosted the evil Shakpi, Hiss wondered at his future. Should he give up? Give in, break with this life and move on to the next? Or should he fight to free himself? Was it important that the ones who imprisoned him now knew why he had turned against them? That it was their own treachery, their callous disregard for his family—and shit, for three of their own—that had brought this about?

The door was pushed open and one of his fellow Hunters, Rosalie, appeared. She was in her human form and she could barely look him in the eye as she announced that a visitor had come to see him.

"I don't want to see anyone," he growled. Every second he breathed, his shame grew like a cancer.

"What you want doesn't matter anymore,"

Rosalie said, before motioning to whoever was behind her to come inside.

Only days ago, Hiss had stood sentry outside that door. In his quest for revenge, he'd fallen so far down it would be impossible to crawl back up. He knew that, knew he was done for, and he didn't want anyone else in his face telling him so.

A female with green eyes and dark hair pulled back into a ponytail stepped into the room. She wasn't remotely tall, but there was a toughness about her, a sharpness that didn't suffer fools well.

Hiss turned to the Hunter near the door. "You can go, Rosalie. I'm not about to paw my visitor."

"Not a chance, Hiss." This time her eyes met his, and they were filled with hot, raw disappointment.

It was a look that scratched at Hiss's insides, that snaked into the very core of his own Hunter nature and bit at shards of his remaining moral compass. He pulled his gaze from her and settled it on the female in front of him. "Who are you and what do you want?"

Her green eyes narrowed. Not with malice, but with keen interest. "Do you remember me?"

"I believe we've met before," Hiss answered caustically. "Sebastian's mate, right?"

The female nodded. "But that's not all I am, it seems."

"Why do I care?" He couldn't imagine why the female was here, what she wanted from him.

She took a deep breath and let it out. "Before coming here I really didn't know what I was. I knew I wasn't like the other humans I worked with, was friends with, but I didn't really try and go digging for answers." Her eyes softened. "Until Sebastian."

Hiss cursed and dropped down on the cot. "Have you come here to tell me about your perfect little love story, Female? Because that would be a true form of torture for me."

"Sebastian wanted to know who I was, where I'd come from, how a Pantera female could grow up among the humans without anyone ever looking for me," she continued, unfazed by his vicious attitude. "He took a hair sample from me." She grimaced. "Without me knowing about it—"

Hiss growled. "Get on with it, Female. I have all day and night, true, but not for this pointless bullshit."

Her face fell. "The sample was tested, and DNA—my DNA—matched another shifter here in the Wildlands."

Something hot and aching rolled through Hiss at her words. Why the hell was she here? What kind of game were the Pantera playing? Or maybe this was the elders—

"I'm your sister, Hiss."

The words popped out of her mouth like bullets from a gun. At first, Hiss wasn't sure he'd heard it correctly. Then he replayed it. Again. And again in his mind.

"You're lying," he uttered tersely, coming to his feet.

"No." She shook her head.

"That's impossible. My sister is dead. My parents are dead. I have no family."

Tears pricked in her green eyes and she shrugged. "I don't know how this happened, how we got separated. If our parents are truly gone, or what. But DNA tests don't lie. I'm your blood, Hiss." She lifted her chin. "I'm your sister."

ABOUT THE AUTHORS

Alexandra Ivy is a *New York Times* and *USA Today* bestselling author of the Guardians of Eternity series, as well as the Immortal Rogues. After majoring in theatre she decided she prefers to bring her characters to life on paper rather than stage. She lives in Missouri with her family. Visit her website at alexandraivy.com.

New York Times and USA Today Bestselling Author, **Laura Wright** is passionate about romantic fiction. Though she has spent most of her life immersed in acting, singing and competitive ballroom dancing, when she found the world of writing and books and endless cups of coffee she knew she was home. Laura is the author of the bestselling Mark of the Vampire series and the USA Today bestselling series, Bayou Heat, which she co-authors with Alexandra Ivy.

Laura lives in Los Angeles with her husband, two young children and three loveable dogs.

Made in the USA
Coppell, TX
01 February 2022